ISBN 978-1-330-82488-7
PIBN 10110294

This book is a reproduction of an important historical work. Forgotten Books uses
state-of-the-art technology to digitally reconstruct the work, preserving the original format
whilst repairing imperfections present in the aged copy. In rare cases, an imperfection in
the original, such as a blemish or missing page, may be replicated in our edition. We do,
however, repair the vast majority of imperfections successfully; any imperfections that
remain are intentionally left to preserve the state of such historical works.

For support please visit www.forgottenbooks.com

English
Français
Deutsche
Italiano
Español
Português

www.forgottenbooks.com

Mythology Photography **Fiction**
Fishing Christianity **Art** Cooking
Essays Buddhism Freemasonry
Medicine **Biology** Music **Ancient**
Egypt Evolution Carpentry Physics
Dance Geology **Mathematics** Fitness
Shakespeare **Folklore** Yoga Marketing
Confidence Immortality Biographies
Poetry **Psychology** Witchcraft
Electronics Chemistry History **Law**
Accounting **Philosophy** Anthropology
Alchemy Drama Quantum Mechanics
Atheism Sexual Health **Ancient History**
Entrepreneurship Languages Sport
Paleontology Needlework Islam
Metaphysics Investment Archaeology
Parenting Statistics Criminology
Motivational

[See p. 92

"THEY SENT SHELL AFTER SHELL INTO THE VILLAGE"

ADVENTURES OF
UNCLE SAM'S SOLDIERS

BY

GEN. CHARLES KING, JOHN HABBERTON
CAPTAIN CHARLES A. CURTIS
LIEUT. CHARLES D. RHODES
AND OTHERS

ILLUSTRATED

NEW YORK AND LONDON
HARPER & BROTHERS PUBLISHERS
MCMXII

[See p. 9]

"THEY SENT SHELL AFTER SHELL INTO THE VILLAGE"

ADVENTURES OF
UNCLE SAM'S SOLDIERS

BY

GEN. CHARLES KING, JOHN HABBERTON
CAPTAIN CHARLES A. CURTIS
LIEUT. CHARLES D. RHODES
AND OTHERS

ILLUSTRATED

NEW YORK AND LONDON
HARPER & BROTHERS PUBLISHERS
MCMVII

HARPER'S ADVENTURE SERIES

Each Post 8vo, Illustrated, 60 cents.

Here are some of the best tales of adventure which have been written for younger readers of recent years. These stories have been carefully selected with a view to interest and wholesome excitement. They are the kind of stories that hold the reader fast and keep him wondering as to the outcome. They also convey a measure of historical and general information. Each book has one central subject, and each subject is one that is of engrossing interest to younger readers. Some of these books are as follows:

ADVENTURES OF UNCLE SAM'S SAILORS. By COMMANDER R. E. PEARY, U. S. N., MOLLY ELLIOT SEA-WELL, KIRK MUNROE, WILLIAM J. HENDERSON, CAPTAIN ALBION V. WADHAMS, U. S. N., and others.

ADVENTURES OF UNCLE SAM'S SOLDIERS. By GEN. CHARLES KING, JOHN HABBERTON, CAPTAIN CHARLES A. CURTIS, LIEUT. CHARLES D. RHODES, and others.

ADVENTURES WITH INDIANS. By PHILIP V. MIGHELS, W. O. STODDARD, MAJOR G. B. DAVIS, U. S. A., PAUL HULL, and others.

ADVENTURES WITH PIRATES. By REAR-ADMIRAL JOHN H. UPSHUR, G. E. WALSH, JOHN KENDRICK BANGS, R. GOURLEY, and others.

ADVENTURES AT SEA. By REAR-ADMIRAL T. H. STEVENS, F. H. SPEARMAN, WILLIAM J. HENDERSON, and others.

CONTENTS

iii

670

CONTENTS

ILLUSTRATIONS

INTRODUCTION

FOR the most part these stories of brave deeds in army life show the kind of men who guarded our West in the days of hostile Indians. While these tales are usually fiction, yet the fiction is usually founded upon some incident of actual occurrence. The old frontier posts have now disappeared. They were centres of a life of adventure and often of a silent heroism, in which women and children as well as officers and men bore their full share. It was a lonely life, but full of picturesque incident and thrilling experiences, as these pages show. Many adventures of Uncle Sam's soldiers are told in the volumes of *Harper's Strange Stories from History*, which sketch events in our great wars. In the present volume it has seemed peculiarly worth while to afford a glimpse of the soldier's work in clearing the way for civilization upon this continent.

INTRODUCTION

There is the more reason for this because the courage and endurance of the American regular soldier, during the long years of Indian hostilities in the West, has never received just recognition. The British soldier in every corner of the world has been celebrated by poets and story - writers, and he has received substantial rewards from the authorities at home. Many a brave deed by American soldiers in our West, which has passed almost unnoticed, would have given a theme equal to Kipling's subjects, and the heroes were equally deserving of recognition. But the wretched mistakes in our treatment of Indians, due so largely to politicians and dishonest agents, have reacted unfavorably upon those who were simply the instruments of their superiors — upon the American regular soldiers. So much may properly be said, even in an introduction to a story-book which offers, first of all, entertainment. That will be found, assuredly, in these tales of daring, not only in the West, but elsewhere, for there are glimpses of the great war, and also of the stern duty which may devolve upon the soldier when law is set at naught in civil life.

While these are tales for younger readers,

and young actors play a frequent part, it may well happen that this book will tempt some one to look closer into the record of the regular soldiers which is given so inadequately in most histories of our country. The Revolution, with its experiences of Hessian and British regulars, strengthened American distaste for a regular soldiery. Afterwards the army of the United States was reduced almost to the vanishing-point. But the disasters of Harmer and Harmon in the expedition against Chillicothe in 1790, and St. Clair's disastrous defeat the following year, were costly lessons. " However pacific the general policy of a nation may be," wrote Washington in 1796, " it ought never to be without an adequate stock of military knowledge." Happily, our country is pacific, and it is for the younger generation to learn and continue lessons of peace; but that does not diminish the value of a true reading of history. For only a part of the soldier's work has been in war. The great explorers of the West were soldiers, Lewis and Clark, who made their classic journey from St. Louis to the mouth of the Columbia River in 1804-06; Pike, who sought the sources of the Mississippi in 1805, and the following year, travelling westward, reached Pike's Peak, and Frémont, explorer of routes to the Pacific from 1842 to 1853. These are only the most conspicuous examples of the achievements of the soldier in initial path-finding and surveys and reconnoissances. There was also the policing of the old frontier and the guardianship of the great routes known as the Overland, Oregon, and Santa Fé Trails.

As to the wretched decades of Indian warfare, closing only in 1890 with scenes suggested in a story in this book, the arduous, gallant, thankless part of the soldier may be gathered from General G. A. Forsyth's *Thrilling Scenes of Army Life,* and J. P. Dunn's *Massacres of the Mountains.* These and a few other books, particularly General Forsyth's *Story of the Soldier,* record deeds like the march of Kearny and Cooke over 2000 miles from Fort Leavenworth to Santa Fé and the Pacific in 1846-47, the fruitless Utah expedition of 1857 against the Mormons, the Fetterman massacre at Fort Phil Kearny in the Big Horn country in 1866, and the punishment of Red Cloud and his followers by Major Powell the following year; General Forsyth's gallant stand against overwhelming numbers on a fork of the Republican River in Kansas in 1868; the long years of campaigns against hostile Sioux in the north and Apaches in the southwest; the Modoc war in Oregon in 1872; the Custer massacre in 1876, and the wonderful fight of the heroic Chief Joseph and his Nez Percé followers in 1877, which covered some 1500 miles, traversing three great mountain ranges. These are a few of the campaigns and battles in which the American soldier, obeying orders, has done a hero's work in the winning of our West.

A volume like this is, plainly, a small side-light upon history rather than history itself. But facts may be vividly illustrated in fiction, and, in introducing this story-book to American boys and girls, it has seemed worth while to lay stress upon certain facts of our history which have not been justly appreciated.

The regulars who fought to win and guard the West were not responsible for broken treaties, invaded lands, and stolen supplies. Even the hostile Indians recognized the truthfulness of regulars like Crook and Howard. More than this, our greatest soldiers, like Grant, with his prayer for peace, and Sherman, with his denunciation of war, would have chosen to be not instruments of bloodshed, but messengers of peace.

ADVENTURES OF UNCLE SAM'S
SOLDIERS

ADVENTURES OF
UNCLE SAM'S SOLDIERS

RECAPTURED

A Story of the Apache Days in Arizona

THERE was a boy at old Camp Sandy once upon a time when white men were scarce in Arizona. From the day he was ten years old this boy's consuming desire was to help " clean out," as he heard the soldiers express it, a certain band of mountain Apaches who had surprised and slaughtered a small party of people in whose welfare he felt especial interest, for the reason that there was with them a little fellow of his own age. They had been at Sandy only three days, and then, deaf to remonstrance, had gone on their way up into the mountains "prospecting"; but during those three days the two youngsters had been insep- arable. "Sherry" Bates, the sergeant's son, had done the honors of the post for Jimmy Lane, the miner's boy; had proudly exhibited the troop quarters, stables, and corrals; had taken him across the stream to the old ruins up the opposite heights, and told him prodigious stories of the odd people that used to dwell there; had introduced him personally to all the hounds, big and little, and had come to grief in professing to be on intimate terms with a young but lively black bear cub at the sutler's store. He was rescued from serious damage from bruin's claws and clasping arms only by the prompt dash of by-standers. It took some of Sherry's conceit out of him, but not all, and the troopers had lots of fun, later on, at the corral, when he essayed to show Master Jim how well he could ride bare-back, and mounted one of Mexican Pete's little "burros" by way of illustration.

All the same, they were days of thrilling in- terest, and Sherry wept sorely when, a week later, a friendly Indian came in and made known to the officers, mainly by signs, that the

4

party had been killed to a man, that their mutilated bodies were lying festering in the sun about the ruins of their wagons up near Stoneman's Lake in the pine country of the Mogollon.* The major commanding sent out a scouting party to investigate, and the report proved only too true. The bodies could no longer be identified; but one thing was certain: there were the remains of four men, hacked and burned beyond recognition, but not a trace of little Jim.

"It was Coyote's band, beyond doubt," said the lieutenant who went in command, and for Coyote's band the troopers at Sandy "had it in," as their soldier slang expressed it, for long, long months—for over a year, in fact—before they ever got word or trace of them. They seemed to have vanished from the face of the earth. Meantime there had been chase after chase, scout after scout. General Crook had been transferred long since to another field, and was busy with the Sioux and Cheyennes. Another commander, one who lacked Crook's knowledge of Indian tricks and character, had taken charge in Arizona, and the Apaches had

* Pronounced Mogol*yone.*

5

quickly found it out. They made it lively for small parties, and easily kept out of the path of big ones. And this was the way things were going when, one autumn night, signal fires were discovered ablaze away up in the Red Rock country, and Major Wheeler sent a troop post‑haste to see what it meant. With this troop went Sergeant Bates, and on its trail, an hour later, unbeknown to almost everybody, went Sherry.

Indians rarely ventured into the deep valley of the Sandy. The boy had hunted jack-rabbits and shot California quail, and fished for "shiners" and other inconspicuous members of the finny tribe along its banks, and he knew the neighborhood north, south, and west for miles. Eastward, out of sight of the flag-staff, he had never ventured. That was towards the land of the Apache, and thither his father had told him no one could go safely. An only son was Sherry, and a pretty good boy, as boys go, especially when it is considered that he had been motherless for several years.

The old sergeant, his father, watched him carefully, taught him painstakingly, and was very grateful when any of the officers or their wives would help with the lessons of the little

man. He had had a pony to ride, but that pony
was old when his father bought him from an
officer who was ordered to the East, and Sherry
soon declared him too old and stiff for his use.
What he craved was a horse, and occasionally
the men let him mount some of their chargers
when the troop went down to water at the river,
and that was Sherry's glory. On this particular October night he had stolen from his
little bed and made his way to the corral, and
had got Jimmy Lanigan, the saddler sergeant's
son, now a trumpeter in " F " Troop, to saddle
for him a horse usually ridden by Private
McPhee, now sick in hospital of mountain
fever. As Mac couldn't go, his horse would not
be needed, and Sherry determined to ride in
his place.

But some one gave old Bates the " tip," and
he caught the little fellow by the ear and led
him home just before the troop started, and
bade him stay there; and Sherry feigned to be
penitent and obedient, but hugged his father
hard, and so they parted.

But boys who own dogs know the old dog's
trick. Sometimes when starting for a day's
pleasuring where Rover would be very much in
the way, the master has sternly ordered him

home when, with confident joy, the usually welcome pet and companion came bounding and barking after. You have all seen how sad and crestfallen he looked, how dumbly he begged, how reluctantly he skulked homeward when at last he had to go or be pelted with stones; and then, time and again, he finally turned and followed, a long distance behind, never venturing to draw near, until, so very far from home that he knew he couldn't be sent back, he would reappear, tail on high and eyes beaming forgiveness and assurance, and the battle was won.

And Sherry had learned Rover's little game, and he lay patiently in wait until he knew the troop was gone, then over to the corral he stole, easily coaxed the stable sentry into giving him a lift, and in half an hour he was loping northward along the winding Sandy under the starry skies, sure of overtaking the command before the dawn if need be, yet craftily keeping well behind the hindermost, so that his stern old father could not send him back when at last his presence was discovered.

For, long before daybreak, the soldiers were trailing in single file, afoot and leading their horses up the steep, rocky sides of the Mogollon, taking a short-cut across the range instead of following the long, circuitous route to Stoneman's Lake, and only a hundred feet or so behind the rearmost of the pack-train followed keen-eyed, quick-eared, little Sherry, still clinging to his saddle, for his light weight made little difference to such a strong horse as McPhee's Patsy. He trusted mainly to Patsy's power as a trailer to carry him unerringly in the hoof-prints of the troop.

When at last the sun came peering over the pine crests to the east, the little command was deep down in a rocky cañon, and here the captain ordered the men to halt, lead into line, and unsaddle. The horses and the pack-mules were quickly relieved of their loads, and the men were gathering dry fagots for little cook-fires—fires that must make no smoke at all, even down in that rocky defile, for Indian eyes are sharp as a microscope. Before they marched on again, men and horses both had to have their bite, and the men their tin mug of soldier coffee, and here it was that some one suddenly exclaimed:

" Well, I'm blessed if here ain't Sherry!"

It was useless for the old sergeant to scold now. The officers promptly and laughingly took the boy's part and declared him " a chip

9

of the old block," and bade the sergeant bring the boy along. It was safer, at all events, than sending him back.

And so, secretly proud of him, though openly declaring he would larrup him well the moment they got back to the post, Sergeant Bates obeyed his captain, and thus it happened that Master Sherry was with " F " Troop the chill October morning, just at dawn, when they found out, entirely to their satisfaction, just what those signal-fires meant.

They were not visible from Camp Sandy, you must understand. Indians are too sharp for that. They were started in certain deep clefts in the Red Rocks, which permitted their glare to be seen only from the southeast or the east, the direction from which the roving bands approached when seeking to steal their way back to the old reservation after some bloody foray, sure of food and welcome at the lodges of their friends and fellow-savages, provided they came not empty-handed. Coyote's band had not been near the reservation since their exploit of the year before. A price was on the leader's head, but scouting parties away down to the southeast in the Chiricahua country had learned that recently Coyote, with some forty

10

followers, had crossed to the north of the Gila, and seemed to be making his way back to his old haunts in the Mogollon. All this was wired to Major Wheeler, who sent some trustworthy Apache-Mohave scouts out towards the head-waters of Chevelon's Fork to the east, with orders to watch for the coming of Coyote. It was one of these runners who brought in the tidings that the signal-fires were burning, and that meant, " Come on, Coyote; the coast is clear."

And Apache confederates, watching from the reservation, twenty miles up - stream, would have said the coast was still clear, for the road to Stoneman's Lake was untrodden. A day afterwards, to be sure, they got word that a whole troop of horse had gone by night into the mountains, but it was then too late to undo what they had done—lured Coyote many a mile towards his enemies. They sent up " smokes " in the afternoon to warn him, but by that time Coyote's people, what was left of them, knew more than did their friends at the reservation.

For, early that morning, just at dawn, while some of them were sound asleep in their brush shelters, or " wickie-ups," away on top of a rocky pinnacle that overlooked the country for miles, this is what happened:

Following the lead of three or four swart, black-haired, beady-eyed Apache scouts, the soldiers came stealthily climbing the steep. Away down in a rocky cañon they had left the horses and pack-mules, their blankets, and, many of them, their boots, and in moccasins, or even stocking feet in a few cases, they noiselessly made their way. Officers and all carried the death-dealing little brown cavalry carbine, and thimble belts of copper cartridges were buckled about their waists. "Find um top," the leader of the little squad of scouts muttered to the captain, as he pointed the evening before to this distant peak, and well he knew their ways, for only three years before he himself had been a "hostile," who was tamed into subjection by General Crook. And so it proved. Relying on the far-away night fires, Coyote and his weary band had made their brush shelters on the old Picacho. The few squaws with them had filled their water-jars at the cañon. Two trusty runners had gone on westward to the reservation, and the rest betook themselves to sleep. Coyote thought the white soldiers "too heap fool" to think of making a night march through the mountains instead of coming away around by the old road.

With the troop-horses was left a small guard, and with the guard a little boy—Master Sherry Bates—fretting and fuming not a little as he lay there among the rocks, wrapped in his father's blanket, and listening with eagerness unspeakable for the crash of musketry away up on that dimly outlined peak which would tell that his father and the boys had found their foemen and the fight was on. Presently, as the eastern sky began to change from crimson to gold, the lofty summit seemed to blaze with glistening fire. The light, still dim and feeble in the jagged ravine, grew sharp and clear along the range, and one of the guard, peering through the captain's binocular, swore he could " see some of the fellers climbing close to the top "; and Sherry, though shivering with cold and excitement, rolled out of his blanket and scrambled to his feet.

An instant more, and, floating on the mountain breeze, there came the sudden crash and splutter of distant musketry, and Sherry could control himself no longer. Mad with excitement, he began dancing about the bivouac. The men were all listening and gazing. The horses were snorting and pawing. Half shrouded by the lingering darkness in the gorge, he stole away among the stunted pine and went speeding as though for dear life up the cañon.

The fight itself was of short duration. Surprised in their stronghold, the Indians sprang to their arms at the warning cry of one haplessly wakeful sentinel. It was his death-song, too, for Sergeant Bates and the veteran corporal at his side, foremost with the guides, fired together at the dark figure as it suddenly leaped between them and the sky, tumbling the sentry in his tracks. Then, before the startled band could spring to the shelter of surrounding bowlders, the soldiers with one volley and a ringing cheer came dashing in among them. Some warriors, in their panic, leaped from the ledge and were dashed upon the rocks below; some, like mountain-goats, went bounding down the eastward side and disappeared among the straggling timber; some, crouching behind the bowlders, fought desperately, until downed by carbine butt or bullet. Some few wailing squaws knelt beside their slain, sure that the white soldiers would not knowingly harm them; while others, like frightened does, darted away into the shelter

14

of rock or stunted pine. One little Indian boy sat straight up from a sound sleep, rubbing his baby eyes, and yelling with terror. Another little scamp, with snapping black eyes, picked up a gun and pulled the trigger like a man, and then lay sprawling on his back, rubbing a damaged shoulder, and kicking almost as hard as the old musket. And then, while some soldiers went on under a boy lieutenant in chase of the fleeing Indians, others, with their short-winded captain, counted up the Indian losses and their own, and gave their attention to the wounded; and all of a sudden there went up a shout from Sergeant Bates, who was peering over the edge of a shelf of rock.

"Here's more of 'em, sir, running down this way!" followed by a bang from his carbine and a yell from below, and men who reached his side were just in time to see a brace of squaws, dragging two or three youngsters by the hand, darting into the bushes, while their protecting warriors defiantly faced their assailants, fired a shot or two, and then plunged after them. "I know that Indian," almost screamed old Bates. "It's Coyote himself!"

"After 'em, then!" was the order, and away went every man.

15

Two minutes later, out from under a shelving rock came crawling a trembling squaw. Peering cautiously around, and assuring herself the troopers were gone, she listened intently to the sound of pursuit dying away down the mountain-side; then in a harsh whisper summoued some one else. Out from the same shelter, shaking with fear, came a little Apache boy, black and dirty, dragging by the hand another boy, white and dirtier still, and crying. Seizing a hand of each, the woman scurried back along the range, until she reached the narrow trail by which the troopers had climbed the heights; then, panting, and muttering threats to the urchins dragging helplessly after, down the hill-side she tore, but only a hundred yards or so, when, with a scream of fright and misery, she threw herself prone upon her knees before the body of a lithe, sinewy Apache just breathing his last. And then, forgetting her boy charges, forgetting everything for the moment but that she had lost her brave, she began swaying to and fro, crooning some wild chant, while the boys, white and black, knelt shuddering among the rocks in nerveless terror.

And this was the scene that suddenly burst upon the eyes of Sherry, the sergeant's boy, as he came scrambling up the trail in search of his father. And then went up a shrill, boyish voice in a yell of mingled hope and dread and desperation, and the dirty little white savage, screaming "Sherry! Sherry!" went bounding to meet the new-comer. And the squaw rose up and screamed, too—something Master Sherry couldn't understand, but that sent terror to the white boy's heart and lent him wings. "Run! run!" he cried, as he seized Sherry by the hand, and, hardly knowing where they were going, back went both youngsters, tearing like mad down the tortuous trail.

Five minutes later, as some of the men, well-nigh breathless, came drifting in from the pursuit, and Corporal Clancy was running up from the cañon in pursuit of the vanished "kid," both parties stumbled suddenly upon this motley pair, and the rocks rang with Clancy's glad cry.

"Here he is, sergeant! all right, and Jimmy Lane wid him."

And that's why Sherry didn't get the promised larruping when they all got back to Sandy.

A VERY LITTLE FELLOW

Jerry and the Highwaymen

THERE are a great many advantages in being a big fellow; but, on the other hand, there are a number of advantages in being a little fellow. If Jerry had not been a very little fellow, something might have happened that would have been a source of great regret, and this story might never have been written — at least, not about this particular boy.

Aside from all the old-time dangers in our West from Indians and wild animals, there were others, not less to be dreaded, from the lawless characters who took advantage of the difficulty of enforcing the laws of the country. The towns were few and far between, and even in the towns themselves there was little law and order. Occasionally the law-abiding people would attempt to rid themselves of the rough

18

characters, and the latter, driven from their dishonest pursuits in the towns, would go into the open country and become horse-thieves or highwaymen—more commonly known through the West as "road-agents."

Little by little, as the Western country became more thickly settled, these bad characters disappeared, but not entirely. And even now one quite frequently hears of the doings of these men in the wilder localities.

It was in just such a place that the scene of my story is laid. Fort McKay was one of those small, isolated army posts in the Indian country which could only be reached by a long overland trip from the little box of a railroad station over one hundred and fifty miles away. There was a stage—a rickety vehicle, drawn by four lean broncos — which made the long trip twice a week. But the price charged was so high, and the journey was such an uncomfortable one, that people from the army post much preferred to travel in their own ambulance, drawn by four well-fed government mules.

And now I think it time for you to know a little more about Jerry — other than the fact that he was a little fellow. He was the only son—a motherless son—of an old soldier in one of the cavalry regiments, and what he did not know about an army post and army life was not worth knowing. He had had very little care in his bringing up, but in his short life had picked up a good deal of the good, a few of the bad, and a great many of the indifferent traits of Uncle Sam's soldiers. He was never known to spell a word right the first time, and he accounted it a very great accomplishment that he could write his name. On the other hand, Jerry could ride like an Indian, drive a team, or even a " four," with a skilled hand, and assist in packing a mule like a veteran. One could never guess Jerry's age, and as he felt rather sensitive about his small size, one could never persuade him to tell just how old he was. But he was so quick and smart and good - natured that he was a general favorite with all whom he met.

Not many years ago the regiment to which Jerry's father belonged received a change of station; and about the same time one of the numerous troubles with the Indians broke out in the very country to which the regiment was transferred. So Jerry, who, to tell the truth, had never had much affection lavished on his young head, was left with a distant relative at a small Nebraska town through which the train bearing the troops passed, until the new stations of the regiment were made known. Now, three months later, the Indian hostilities had ceased, a part of the regiment was safely housed at McKay, and Jerry was alone at the little railroad station of Bronco, ready to take the overland journey to McKay, if he had to walk. Jerry's confidence in his father was unbounded, and when the latter had written to him to take the train for Bronco on a certain day, Jerry had done so, and had asked no questions.

The two young fellows who managed affairs at Bronco had taken Jerry into their house as a matter of course—in the West one's hospitality is not measured by the size of one's dwelling-place. And here, for two days, Jerry had remained, hoping that something would turn up to help him along towards McKay.

And something did turn up. On the morning of the third day the ambulance from McKay arrived at the station, with Lieutenant Johnson in charge; and the next train from the East brought Major McGregor, a crusty old bachelor officer of the regiment; Mrs. Johnson and baby, the lieutenant's wife and child; and Dr. Sanborn, a young army surgeon from the East, who was about to join his first army post at McKay.

In spite of a certain amount of grumbling on the part of the major, who did not like boys of Jerry's age, the latter readily obtained permission to ride on the ambulance with the driver, and the party started across the rough country in high spirits. Jerry waved a very enthusiastic farewell to his railroad friends with what remained of a soiled pocket-handkerchief; Davie, the teamster, cracked his long whip, and the ambulance moved smoothly along over the prairies, leaving in its wake a cloud of thick, white dust.

The trip proceeded during the first day without incident. The country consisted of rolling cattle-ranges, with no fences, trees, or cultivated land to be seen in any direction. The only signs of life were occasional bunches of range-cattle and the ever-present prairie-dogs.

As it became cooler, Davie wrapped his extra blanket about Jerry's small body, and the two huddled together for warmth. Jerry had received too many hard knocks during his lifetime to make a fuss about a little cold.

The first night was spent at a large ranch-house, surrounded with cottonwood-trees, from which could be seen the mountains — on the eastern slope of which Fort McKay was situated. On the following day the journey was resumed, bright and early. The country became rougher, and to the right of the long, winding road the Bad Lands, in all their ugly barrenness, rose into view.

It was a long day's journey—made necessary in order to arrive at the expected stopping-place before nightfall. But the road was rougher than was anticipated, and late in the evening the ambulance was still a long distance from the end of the day's journey, and the weary mules required an occasional touch from the long whip to keep them up to the steady gait.

And this was the time that something happened.

As the ambulance passed over a small divide, and began the descent on the other side, two horsemen galloped up from the timber which fringed the base of the hill, while a third rider moved out to the right and circled towards them from the side.

" Road-agents!" softly whispered Jerry, in

suppressed excitement, and Davie, the teamster, laughed.

But whether it was the instinct of self-preservation or something else, Jerry had slid down beneath the seat and was lost to view. Davie continued to chuckle to himself.

An instant later and Jerry had poked his head up on the inside of the ambulance, between the major's knees, much to that worthy's surprise, for he had begun to doze.

" What in the name of all that's good is this ?" gasped the major.

An ambulance with four grown persons and a baby inside is not a very roomy place at its best, and when Jerry's small body was squeezed in, it created a surprise, for the leather sides of the vehicle had been battened down to keep out the night air, and made it very dark.

" 'Sh !" said Jerry, in a stage - whisper. " Road-agents ahead. Give me your money, quick, and I'll hide." 'And suiting his action to the word, Jerry began to grope around for whatever he might find of value.

The major began to splutter, and the baby began to cry.

" You young scamp," he began, " to come in here in this manner and attempt to alarm a

24

lady—and a—a baby!" with a look in the direction of the howling child.

But the others did not laugh. They were impressed by Jerry's earnestness.

Just then, however, a gruff voice was heard in front. The ambulance came to a sudden stop, and another voice called to the driver: "Hands up! Come down from there!"

Then it was that the passengers, the major excepted, fully realized what had happened, and valuables were thrust into Jerry's broad-brimmed hat in less time than it takes to tell it. Two rolls of greenbacks, three watches, some rings, and a diamond pin were among the articles, and just as a rough hand turned the knob of the ambulance door, Jerry, with his precious hat, rolled under the hangings of the front seat out of sight.

"Climb out of here!" yelled a fierce-looking man with a red handkerchief tied over his face to conceal his features. And he poked the muzzles of two revolvers under the major's nose.

Then, and not till then, did the incredulous major realize that he had really been "held up" by highwaymen; and as he was nearest the door, he was the first to climb awkwardly but quickly down on to the ground and hold up his hands.

Resistance was useless. The others were forced to alight, and while two of the robbers covered the party with their revolvers, the third searched them for valuables.

The search was not pleasant to the major. His arms were getting tired, and he incautiously allowed one of them to drop. He had no sooner done so, however, than one of the desperadoes fired his pistol high over the major's head, as a hint of what he might expect if he was not careful. The major took the hint, and straightened up with a jerk.

But the shot had another, very unexpected, effect. The four mules attached to the ambulance were frightened and sprang forward, and in another instant they were speeding along the road at a gallop, glad to be once more travelling towards home and supper.

The robbers took little heed of this occurrence, until, as they failed to find anything of great value on any one except the major, who meekly submitted to being robbed of a large roll of bills, they began to realize that the valuables of the passengers must have been left in the ambulance. Then they sprang on their

"WHILE TWO OF THE ROBBERS COVERED THE PARTY WITH THEIR REVOLVERS, THE THIRD SEARCHED THEM FOR VALUABLES"

horses, spurred them forward, and dashed down the road after the ambulance in the twinkling of an eye.

Meanwhile, as the mules dashed away, Jerry had crawled up on the driver's seat, and seizing the reins with skilful hands, was soon guiding the runaway animals down the long slope and up the hill on the other side. At the top he glanced behind in time to see the highwaymen mount their horses; then the mules dashed down the next hill, and Jerry clung to the reins with all his strength.

Fortunately the road was straight and smooth at this point, and as the moon was rising, objects could be seen for a long distance ahead. Just how long he could keep ahead of the pursuers depended on how fresh their horses might be, for the mules had already had a long trip, and as their fear disappeared they began to slacken their pace.

In the frosty air sounds could be heard for a long distance, and Jerry felt sure, before long, that his pursuers were steadily gaining on him. But he urged the animals on with the whip, hoping that he might soon strike a ranch or meet a friendly face.

But a new danger presented itself. At a

point near at hand the road made a sweeping turn to the left, in order to avoid some jutting spurs of bluffs on the right. Here it seemed apparent that the outlaws would, by moving across country, overtake the ambulance, and this is exactly what they attempted to do. One of the men kept straight along the road, while the other two turned across the level plain, gaining perceptibly at every bound of their wiry mustangs.

Still, Jerry hung to the reins, although his arms were aching from fingers to shoulders, and he felt almost sure that, unless something unforeseen should occur, he would be overtaken. What would become of him he did not know. The pistol-shot which he had heard while he was concealed might have killed one of the party, and the same fate might be awaiting him. He had a confused idea at one time of jumping from the ambulance and concealing himself in the hills, but he gave it up. He would stick to the ambulance and mules, come what might.

What actually did happen was this: As the ambulance approached the bluffs, nearer and nearer, Jerry saw the two men to the left turn suddenly about, and race quite as hard to the rear as they had previously been racing to the front. Another moment, and the cause of their precipitate flight was apparent. A roaring camp fire at the edge of the bluffs, hitherto concealed from view, rose in sight, and by its light Jerry saw white tents, and a dozen of Uncle Sam's soldiers sprawling about, eating supper. Never had the blue uniform, everywhere symbol of law and order, looked so fascinating, and Jerry had to choke down a big lump which insisted on rising in his throat as he realized that he was among friends.

The mules slowed up as they caught sight of the little camp, and brayed loudly. They were answered by a friendly bray from the mules in camp, and in a few seconds more were standing quietly by the bales of hay, impatient for some kind hand to unharness them and give them their supper.

Friendly faces crowded about Jerry, and friendly hands helped him down from the ambulance, for his stiffened arms and legs refused to act as they usually did.

Jerry's story was soon told, and the sergeant in charge of the detachment, which was on its way to the railroad with wagons for commissary stores, hurriedly mounted a few of his men to look for the outlaws — a task which proved, in the end, to be fruitless. The camp mules, too, were quickly harnessed to the ambulance, and several of the soldiers went back after the party which had been so unceremoniously left in the road—a number of miles to the rear. Jerry, his precious hat by his side, sat by the blazing fire, and, between bites of hot supper served on a tin plate, recited over again, for the benefit of the camp cook, the story of his fast drive over the hills.

A couple of hours later the ambulance again appeared, and, crowded as it was, Jerry was taken inside at once, and as the ambulance rumbled along to the ranch near by, he went over the whole affair again.

The ranch was soon reached, and Jerry, you may be sure, was the hero of the hour. He had to eat another supper with his enthusiastic friends; and afterwards, like a game of forfeits, each member of the party, save the major, was called upon to redeem the property which had so hastily been stuffed into Jerry's capacions hat.

"You're a little fellow, Jerry," said the surgeon, "but it's lucky for us in many ways that you have a big head, and consequently a

30

big hat," to which all the others, save the
major and the baby, gave unqualified assent.

The baby was asleep; and the major, disgusted that he had lost his valuables through
his own stupidity, simply looked gloomy.

"I don't care so much about the money,"
said he. "Luckily it did not amount to a great
deal. But there's that watch, an heirloom in
my family for nearly a hundred years — I
wouldn't have lost it for—"

But he did not finish his sentence, and no
one ever knew just what the major would have
said. For, from the moment that he mentioned
the watch, Jerry had been tugging at one of
his tight, little pockets until he was red in the
face.

"I almost forgot," said he, eagerly. And in
another moment, from where it was crowded in
with a soiled handkerchief, an exploded cartridge, a one-bladed knife, and a broken jews-
harp, Jerry dragged forth in triumph the major's missing watch.

"How in the name of all that's good," gasped the delighted major, "did you get it?"

"I took it out of your vest pocket when I
squeezed up between your knees in the ambulance," answered the equally pleased Jerry.

And every one, including the major, agreed that under the circumstances it was a perfectly justifiable case of pocket - picking, and that there are many advantages in being a very little fellow, provided that one has a clear head and a sure hand.

HOW REDDY GAINED HIS COMMISSION

The Story of a Rescue

I

G UARD - MOUNTING was over. The commanding officer in the adjutant's office was occupied with the daily routine business of a frontier post. At tables near him sat the post-adjutant, the acting sergeant - major, and a soldier clerk, writing and making up the semi-weekly mail for the post - office beyond the neighboring river.

Upon a bench outside the door, serving his tour as office orderly, lounged a boy musician. He leaned listlessly against the wall of the building, apparently oblivious to the grandeur of the views around him. To the south, across an undulating plain, seventy miles away, were the twin Spanish Peaks. To the west, the

33

Cuerno Verde range let itself down to the plain by a succession of lesser elevations, terminating in rounded foot-hills, forty miles distant. Eighty miles to the northwest towered the majestic form of Pike's Peak.

The fort was occupied by a troop of cavalry and a company of infantry, the captain of the infantry being in command. This officer was now attaching his signature to various military documents. When the last paper was signed the young orderly entered, and, standing at "attention" before the captain, said:

"Sir, my mother would like to speak to the commander."

"Very well, Maloney; take these papers to the quartermaster and the surgeon, and tell your mother to come in."

The orderly departed, and soon after a ruddy-faced, substantial daughter of Erin entered, her sleeves rolled above her elbows, and her vigorous hands showing the soft, moist, and wrinkled appearance that indicates recent and long-continued contact with the contents of the wash-tub. Dropping a courtesy, she said:

"Can the commanding officer spare me a few minutes of his toime?"

"With pleasure. Sergeant-major, place a
34

chair for Mrs. Maloney," said Captain Bartlett.

"Oi want to spake a worrud about me b'y
Teddy, sor."

"What is it about your son? Does he need
disciplining?"

Seating herself upon the edge of the prof-
fered chair, the Irish woman clasped her moist
hands in her lap, and said:

"Small doubt but he nades disciplining,
captain; but it is of the great danger to his
loife in carryin' th' mail oi want t' spake."

"A mother's nervous fear, perhaps. He's
an excellent horseman. You are not afraid he
will be thrown?"

"Oh, not at ahl, at ahl, sor. He sthicks to
the muel loike a bur-r-r. I belave no buckin'
baste can throw 'im. It's that roarin' river
oi'm afeared of. The min at the hay-camp,
whose business it is to row the mail acrass the
strame, let Teddy and Reddy do it, do ye know,
sor, and oi fear in the prisint stage of the
wather, and the dispisition of the b'yes to be
larkin' in the boat, they'll overset it, and be
dhrowned."

"Are you quite sure the boys use the boat?"
asked the captain.

" Iv'ry mail-day for the last two wakes, sor."

" And you really think them in danger, Mrs. Maloney ? I am sure they both swim."

" That's jist it, sor! They're not contint to row quiately over loike min, but they must thry all sorts of antics with th' boat. ' Rowin' aich other round ' is one of 'em. Whin oi spake about it they says they can swim. Small chance aven a good swimmer would have in that roarin' river, with its quicksands, its snags, and its bars."

" Well, I will order the hay-camp detail to do the boating hereafter, Mrs. Maloney; so you need have no further anxiety."

" Thank you, sor. It's no liss than oi expected from a koindly and considerate gintleman loike th' captain. Oi hope you'll overlook a mother's anxiety and worrimint over her only b'y. It's not mesilf would be interfarin' with the commanding officer's duties, but oi knowed that you niver mint for Reddy and Teddy to be rowin' that bit of a skift, whin it belonged to the min at the hay-camp to do the same. Goodday, sor, and many thanks for your kindness, captain." And with much ceremonious leavetaking the laundress backed out of the office and hurried back to her tubs.

36

"Mr. Dayton," said the commanding officer, "write Corporal Duffy to hereafter allow no person not a member of his party to row the mail-boat across the river, unless he brings authority from this office."

"Yes, sir."

The letter had been written and sealed when Teddy returned, having changed the full-dress coat and helmet of guard-mounting for a blouse, forage-cap, and leather leggings. Nearly an hour before his drum had rattled an exhilarating accompaniment to the fife, as the guard of twelve privates and three non-commissioned officers marched in review and turned off to the guard-house. Now he stood at the door with spurred heels and gauntleted hands, ready to receive the mail-pouch and ride his little zebra-marked mule to the crossing, two miles from the fort.

The sergeant-major handed him the pouch and the letter addressed to the corporal, with this injunction:

"You are to deliver this letter to Corporal Duffy at the hay-camp, and he will give you some instructions which you are to obey carefully."

Slinging the pouch over his shoulder, and

tucking the letter under his waist-belt, the boy went to his mule behind the office, mounted, and rode away. Passing the quartermaster's corral, another boy, similarly attired, and mounted on a piebald mustang, dashed out with a whoop, and the two went cantering down the slope to the meadow below.

Arriving side by side at a soapweed which marked the southern limit of the river-bottom, the boys put their beasts to the height of their speed, and rode for a dead cottonwood which raised its bleached and barkless branches beside the road three hundred yards beyond.

This stretch was raced over every mail-day, with varying victory for horse and mule. To-day the mule reached the tree half a length ahead, and Teddy was consequently in high glee.

"Ah, Reddy, my boy!" he shouted. "Eight times to your six! Better swap that pony for a mule, if you want to stand any chance with Puss!"

"Pshaw! You were nearly a length ahead when we reached the soapweed, and I almost made it up. Bronc can beat Puss any time when they start even."

"I should say so!" with great disdain.

" How about that day when you got off a length and a half ahead, and I led you half a neck at the cottonwood ?"

" You mean the day Bronc got a stone in his shoe ? Of course he couldn't run then."

The two young soldiers rode on at an easy canter, warmly disputing, for the hundredth time, over the merits of their well-matched animals.

Redmond Carter was the fifer, as Edward Maloney was the drummer, of the infantry company. The latter, the son of a laundress, was a graceful and soldierly boy, dark - complexioned, with black eyes and hair, who bestrode his mule with easy confidence, riding like a Cossack. The other boy, a blond-haired, blue-eyed lad of the same age, quite as tall, but more delicately built, showed less reckless activity in the saddle, but he was a fine and graceful equestrian, nevertheless. He had enlisted a year before, in Philadelphia, naming that city as his residence; but certain peculiarities of speech led Captain Bartlett to believe him a New-Englander. He used better language than his fellows, and it seemed he had received good school advantages before entering the army.

For instance, one day when it was Carter's turn to be office orderly, while sitting at the door he overheard Captain Bartlett, who was writing a private letter, ask the adjutant, " How does that Latin quotation run, Dayton —'*Timeo Danaos et dona ferentes,*' or '*Danaos et dona ferentes?*' "

" Blest if I know. We don't waste time on dead languages at the Point, as you college men do. I can give you the equation of a parabola if you want it."

Captain Bartlett did not ask for the equation, or explain his reason for wanting the proper order of the Latin sentence; but, the morning's office work concluded, and the orderly having departed, as he and the adjutant were passing out of the doorway the latter noticed a leaf of a memorandum-pad lodged against the leg of the bench just vacated. A drawing on its surface attracting his attention, he picked it up. It was a very creditable sketch of a huge wooden horse standing within the wall of an ancient city, and a party of Grecian soldiers in the act of descending by a ladder from an opening in its side. Beneath the drawing was written "*Quicquid id est, timeo Danaos et dona ferentes.—Æneid, II., 49.*"

"Here, captain," said Mr. Dayton, handing the paper to the post commander; "here's the answer to your question."

"What—that boy Carter? How does a boy like that come to be a musician in the army?"

"Can't tell. Probably for the same reason that an occasional graduate of a foreign university turns up in the ranks—hard times and want in civil life, and plenty of clothing and food in military life."

"He is indeed a bright boy, and I have noticed a certain refinement of manner and precision of speech not common to men in the ranks. I must inquire about him."

The two "music boys," Teddy and Reddy, were fast friends and constant companions. They made common cause in all quarrels and disputes, and to ill-treat one was to ill-treat both. Teddy was frequently in trouble, and his friend often pleaded for him at headquarters. Indeed, the adjutant frequently declared that "but for that rampageous young Celt, Carter would never be in trouble." He was quiet by nature, and punctilious in the observance of the most exacting requirements of discipline; while Teddy, through carelessness, was now and then subjected to punishment. Mrs.

Maloney, while bestowing a tender mother's love upon her darling son, entertained a kindly regard, mingled with great respect, for his friend, and looked after Reddy's clothing and belongings quite as carefully as after Teddy's.

Reddy divided the duty of mail-carrier and office orderly with his fellow-musician, yet it rarely happened that one rode without the other's company. An indulgent corralmaster had obtained the consent of the quartermaster to allow two " surplus animals " to be used exclusively by the boys, provided they would take care of them.

On reaching the river the boys drew up before two tents pitched in a small grove of cottonwoods upon the grassy bank, and occupied by a corporal and three privates, whose duty it was to keep the cattle of the neighboring ranchmen from trespassing upon the meadows of the military reservation.

The lads dismounted, Teddy going to the corporal's tent to deliver the adjutant's letter. But the corporal was not in, having gone with two of his men to drive some cattle out of the bottom.

" I will take the letter to Corporal Duffy, Ted," said Redmond, " while you row over with the mail-bag. Row well up stream before you attempt to cross, so as not to get sucked into the rapids."

" All right," replied the orderly; " and when I come back we'll see which can row the other round."

" That's already settled. I rowed you round the last two times," said Reddy.

" Yes; one day when my wrist was lame, and the other when I had cut my thumb."

" Anything ail you to-day?"

" I believe not."

" Then we will try it again; and be sure if I row you round, you are not to lay your defeat to sprains, cuts, or rheumatism."

Redmond remounted his pony and started into the meadow, while Teddy, having picketed his mule, stepped into a neat wherry tied to the bank. He was not unconscious that he was disobeying orders, for his mother had told him the result of her interview with the commanding officer; but the order was not officially published, and he wanted to have one last pull on the river.

It was in July, the season of freshets in streams having their sources in the Rocky Mountains, when the warmer the weather the faster the snows melt and the deeper and more rapid the stream. The silt-laden current swept swiftly down the middle stream, swelling into rolling waves, which caught the soldier boy's oars as the boat rose on their crests and sank in their troughs.

Reaching the other side, he carried the mail-pouch to the overland stage station, and returned to the boat. Repeating the precaution of rowing up stream before venturing to cross, he arrived at the tents just as Reddy returned from an unsuccessful search for the corporal.

The adjutant's letter was left in the tent, Bronc picketed, and the boys drew lots for the oars. Teddy won the choice, and selected the bow. The contest was to maintain an even-time stroke, and see which could turn the boat toward his opponent — " pull him round," as the phrase is.

Barefooted, barelegged, bareheaded, and coatless, the boys stepped into the boat. Confident in their united strength, they did not row up the eddy, but pulled directly from the shore, beginning the struggle from the start. The wherry leaped ahead, refusing to turn to the right or left. The boys were evidently as well matched as their mounts, Puss and Bronc.

"THERE WAS A CRACKING OF TACKLE, AND JERRY SWINGING IN FROM THE YARD-ARM"

The boat rose and fell in the current waves, and the oars tripped and splashed in the roily crests, until there suddenly came a sharp snap, and Teddy fell backward, holding aloft the bladeless half of an oar. Reddy ceased rowing; the skiff lost headway and floated down the river.

In the confusion of the accident neither boy saw a threatening danger. In the middle of the river was the trunk of a dead cottonwood, standing at an angle of forty-five degrees, its roots firmly anchored to the bottom. The boat floated against the snag, striking amidships. Its starboard side rose, its port side lowered, the water poured over the gunwale, and in an instant Teddy was clinging to the trunk, and Reddy swimming in the boiling current. The boat hung for a moment, as if undecided whether to drop to the right or left of the snag, twisting and struggling in the fierce tide, and at last slid off astern and floated away downstream.

A foot above the water was a large knot and a swell in the trunk of the tree. Teddy climbed above this, and sat astride of it, clasping the trunk in his arms. He was at first inclined to treat the accident with bravado, and he waved

45

a hand above his head and shouted; but the sight of Reddy floating towards the rapids froze his utterance and paralyzed his arm.

It was plainly impossible for his comrade to swim to the shore—he was too near the dangerons fall—but he hoped he might reach the jam in the middle of its crest.

II

WHEN Reddy found himself in the water, he realized the impossibility of swimming to the shore, and began to struggle in an effort to reach the jam. This jam had its origin in a group of sandstone bowlders in the centre of the river, on the edge of the rapids. The river débris had collected and compacted about them into several square yards of solid surface. To the corporal and his fellow-soldiers, now gathered on the shore and watching the swimmer, it seemed that the boy must be carried past to certain death.

They were ready to give him up for lost when they saw him snatch at a branch attached to the edge of the jam and swing himself about, then reach a protruding log and climb out.

Instantly he ran to the outer end of the log and reached his floating oar. With the oar he caught the prow of the boat, and swinging it within reach of his hand, drew it out of the water.

The soldiers gazed at the stranded boys in perplexity. There seemed no chance of rescuing them. They knew of no other boat nearer than the next government post, nor would a raft be of use at the head of the roaring fall. The stream was too deep for wading and too near the plunge for swimming. The corporal quickly mounted the mule and rode to the fort to report the lad's plight to the commanding officer.

As soon as possible an ambulance containing the officers and Mrs. Maloney started for the river. They brought some tools, a spare oar, and several coils of rope. A few moments later nearly all the men of the garrison not on duty lined the southern shore. Mrs. Maloney's worst fears seemed to be realized when she saw her son clinging helplessly to the snag in midstream. Her anguish was heartrending.

" Ah, Teddy b'y !" she screamed, oblivious to the fact that he could not hear her voice above

47

the roar of the water, " don't ye let go the tray, darlint! Howld on till hilp gets t' yez!"

But how to get to them, or to get anything to them, was a serious question. The soldiers were brave and willing men, but they did not possess the skill of river-drivers nor the appliances and tools of the craft. If the boys were only a mile farther up stream, clear of the rapids, a score of swimmers could take lines out to them; or, for that matter, the boys could swim ashore without assistance. The close vicinity of the snag to the plunging and tumultuous descent in the river made all the difference.

Experiment after experiment was tried. Several brave fellows in turn tied the end of the rope to their waists and swam out; but the current pulling at the slack between them and the shore drew them back. Another went far up stream and swam out, while the shore end of the rope was carried down by comrades at the same rate as the flow of the current. He succeeded in grasping the snag; but the instant he paused the titanic force of the water tore him away, burying him beneath the surface. He was drawn ashore and nearly drowned.

The commanding officer was about to send to

the fort for material for a raft and an anchor, when his attention was called to the boy on the jam. After the failure of the last attempt to rescue his friend, Reddy was seen to approach the boat and launch it. He then drew it to the end of the log previously mentioned, held it by the stern, with the prow pointed downward, and appeared to be looking for a passage through the submerged bowlders. Presently he turned towards his friends on shore, swung the oar over his head, stepped on board, and was quickly out of sight.

A cry of alarm went up from the soldiers when Reddy disappeared, and they with one accord started on a run down the shore. At the foot of the steep descent they found the brave soldier boy paddling his skiff into a quiet eddy.

He was greeted with vociferous enthusiasm, and a dozen men shouldered him and the boat, and carried them back to the landing. There a line was attached to the stern of the skiff, and a strong man rowed out towards the snag, but the current dragged it back precisely as it had the swimmers. Captain Bartlett next ordered the boat to be towed a quarter of a mile up stream, and as it floated down and was rowed outward he directed the shore end of the line to be carried along with it.

It became quickly evident to the spectators that the skiff would reach the snag, and an involuntary cheer went up, Mrs. Maloney waving her apron and screaming with tearful joy. But through some blunder, or lack of skill, the original accident was repeated. The wherry dropped sideways against the tree and was swamped. This time, however, a line being attached, the skiff was drawn free, and swung back to the shore by the pull of the current. The man clung to the boat and was landed at the crest of the rapid.

The anguish of the poor mother at the failure of what had promised to be a certain rescue of her son was pitiful. She fell upon her knees, wrung her hands, and sobbed in abject despair. Reddy approached, stooped beside her, and placing an arm about her neck, said:

"Do not cry, Mrs. Maloney; I'm going to ask the captain to let me go to Teddy, and I'll have him here with you in no time."

"No, no, child. Don't ye be dhrowned, too. Nothing can save me b'y, now ahl the min have failed."

"But I mean to try it, Mrs. Maloney. Dry your tears and watch me do it."

Teddy Maloney, on the snag in mid-stream, was now suffering intensely. Seated upon a tree trunk barely ten inches in diameter, and kept from slipping down its slope by a rugged knot, his position was almost unendurable. For five hours he had clung there, hatless and coatless, with his back to a broiling sun. Dazed by suffering and dizzied by the leaping, gliding, and wrinkling water that gurgled and pulled at his half-submerged legs, he was still conscious of the efforts being made for his rescue. He saw Reddy shoot the rapids, and with a growing conviction that he could not hold on much longer, he wondered why his boy friend did not come to his aid. "He is the only one in the whole crowd that knows anything about a boat. Why don't they let him do something?" thought poor Teddy.

As if in answer to this silent appeal, Redmond Carter at the same moment approached Captain Bartlett and begged permission to go for his comrade.

"But, Carter, how can you expect to accomplish what these older and stronger men have failed to do?" asked the captain.

"They do not know what to do, sir. I was born on the Kennebec, sir. I have run barefooted on booms, rafts, and jams, and have boated in birch canoes, dugouts, punts, and yawls, and I can run a rapid, as you have just seen."

"A Kennebec boy, Reddy!" said the officer, for the first time using the boy's pet name. "I know what Kennebec boys could do when I was one of them. You may try it; but be careful."

Reddy sprang into the boat and began rowing up stream in the shore eddy. Reaching the desired distance he turned into the middle of the river, and, changing his seat to the stern and using an oar for a paddle, he dropped down the current towards the snag. As he neared it, he saw Teddy's hands relax and his body sway slightly to the right.

"Hold on, Teddy!" he shouted. "Keep your grip! I'm right here!"

Gliding along the right side of the trunk he stayed the motion of the skiff by grasping it with his left hand.

"Tumble in, Teddy—quick!" he said.

Teddy obeyed, literally falling into the bottom of the boat, limp and sprawling between the thwarts.

Reddy let go the trunk and went towards the rapids, taking the crest at the same place he had taken it before. Down, down the boiling, foaming, roaring descent he sped, plying his oar with all his might, lest in turning a frothing Scylla he might be hurled upon a thundering Charybdis. His former success attended him.

Again the soldiers ran to meet him at the foot of the watery slope, filling the air with shouts as they ran. But the sight of Teddy lying senseless in the bottom of the boat checked further joyous demonstration. He was tenderly lifted in stalwart arms and borne to a grassy knoll near by, where he was received by his anxious mother and the surgeon. Restorative treatment brought him back to consciousness, and he was taken at once to the fort. The wherry was again carried to the landing before the hay-camp, and the crowd of soldiers dispersed through the ravines and groves in the direction of their barracks.

Captain Bartlett accompanied Redmond Carter to the place where the mule and pony were picketed, and, saying that he would ride Puss to the post, ordered one of the men to saddle her, and entered into conversation with the boy.

5
53

" I think you are out of place in the army, Carter," said he.

" What, sir! Have I not always done my duty well?" asked Reddy, in dismay.

" Much better than the average soldier. But that is not what I mean. You seem qualified for something better than the position you occupy. You are not of the material from which the army is usually recruited. This slip of paper, found beside the orderly bench at the office," observed the officer, handing the boy his sketch of the Trojan horse with the accompanying Latin sentence, " shows that you have been a student. I do not know what accident brought you here, but I think school is the proper place for you."

" Nothing would please me better, sir, than to be able to return to school; but it is not possible at present."

" Are you willing to tell me how you come to be in the service?"

" Yes, sir; it is not a long story," replied the young soldier. " My father and mother died when I was too young to remember them, and I was left to the care of a guardian, who sent me to school, and afterwards to an academy, where I prepared for college. I passed my entrance examination to the freshman class in June, and expected to go on in September; but the failure of companies in which my property had been invested left me destitute, and I gave it up."

"But you have relatives?"

"Lots of them; but they showed little inclination to help me. There had been some family differences that I never understood, and I was too proud to go begging for assistance. I shipped on a granite-schooner for Philadelphia. I was miserably seasick the whole trip, and was discharged by the master of the vessel without pay. Having no money I could not find food while looking for work. I obtained an odd job now and then, but soon wore my clothes to rags, so that no respectable establishment would think of hiring me. I slept on the streets, and frequently passed a day without proper food. One day I passed a recruiting-office, and it suggested a means of escape from destitution. I enlisted as a fifer, and was assigned to your company."

"And you have been with me ten months," said the captain. "I suppose your relatives cannot trace you?"

"They might trace me to Philadelphia," replied Reddy; "but the trail becomes dark there. Even if they suspected I had enlisted —which is not likely—they could not find me, for the recruiting sergeant blundered in registering my name. He put me down as Redmond A. Carter, when he should have written it Raymond J. Corser."

"Not a rare mistake of the recruiting officer. So you are of the General Corser family?"

"He was my grandfather."

"Then you have only to communicate with your relatives in order to get out of the army. Yours is an influential family."

"I shall serve out my enlistment, sir. The army has served me a good turn, and when I am discharged I shall be in better condition to find employment than in Philadelphia."

"But what has become of your college aspirations?"

"It will still be possible to accomplish that. Sergeant Von Wold and I are studying together, and I think I shall be able to enter sophomore. Poor boys have worked their way before."

"I have noticed Von Wold. Is he a scholar?"

"Please not to mention it, sir; he is a German university man. When I am discharged I shall have most of my five years' pay, and considerable savings on clothing not drawn. I expect it will amount to nearly eight hundred dollars."

For a few moments the officer said nothing, but gazed reflectively across the rushing and roaring river. At last he turned again towards the boy and asked, "How would you like to be an officer in the army, Carter?"

"I should like it above all things, sir; but it is not possible. While I might make a struggle single-handed through college, I could scarcely hope to secure an appointment to West Point."

"Still there is a way. The late Congress passed a law allowing men who have served two years in the army, and been favorably recommended by their officers, to be examined for appointment to the grade of second lieutenant. You have a little more than four years to serve. In that time you will have reached the required age, and Lieutenant Dayton and I can give you the necessary instruction. What do you say?"

"I'll make a hard struggle for it, sir, if you will afford me the chance."

Five years later Sergeant Redmond A.

Carter passed a successful examination for a second lieutenancy in the army, and was commissioned in the artillery under his proper name, Raymond J. Corser.

Edward Maloney, who excelled in physical rather than intellectual attainments, continued in the service, becoming at the time of his second enlistment first sergeant of Captain Bartlett's company.

AT THE HELIO STATION

The Capture of Alchise

FOR two months L Troop of the Third United States Cavalry had been chasing Alchise and his band of hostile Apaches over the roughest ground in the world—the Sierra Mogollon of southeastern Arizona. Alchise was a negroid half-breed, and had been one of Geronimo's lieutenants, in which capacity he had fought General Crook, and had considerably excelled his superior officer in ingenious atroeities. The traces of his progress that L Troop frequently encountered were such as to convince them that he had lost none of his wickedness with years. Yet for nearly nine weeks it had been impossible to come to closer quarters with the hostiles than a telescopic glimpse of a dirt-brown figure skulking among the rocks a mile away, or a long-range rifle slug dropped scientifically into the camp at about a thousand yards.

At last, however, success seemed within reach. The friendly Apache scouts with the column reported that the enemy had established a *ranchesia* deep in a defile of the San Francisco range, where there were warriors, and women, and children, and numerous pits in which fires were built to stew the leaves of the *maguey* plant, from which an intoxicating drink is made called *mescal*. It was fifty miles away, and Troop L advanced carefully in that direction, moving chiefly at night, and never lighting so much as a match, except under a tented screen of blankets. Then lest the enemy should escape at the eleventh hour, they left a detail of signallers on the top of the Yellow Butte, with orders to report by beacon fire if at night, and by heliograph if by day, should they discern any sign of Indians upon the landscape. This signal-station was twenty miles from the column's line of march, and there was a second station upon a peak more directly in touch with the fighting-line, to receive messages.

Lieutenant Ward Howell was in charge of the heliograph post, and he had with him four troopers and an Apache scout. A small A-tent afforded shelter for himself and for the signalling instrument, and the troopers built a rampart of rough bowlders all around the tent, except upon the east, where the ground dropped five hundred feet straight to the brown 'dobe desert that ran flat to the eastern sky-line.

There had been no sign of any enemy from the pines on the peaks to the cacti on the plains, and on the third evening they were rolled unexpectantly in their blankets about nine o'clock, when Lieutenant Howell was aroused by the sentry's challenge. He sprang up to see, by the starlight and the gleam of a small fire in the enclosure, a short, thick-set Indian parleying with the sentinel, who was barring the way.

"Who's that, Connolly, and what does he want?" demanded the lieutenant.

"It's a 'Pache, for sure,. sorr," replied the trooper, richly. "An' I'm thinkin' he do want to talk to yerself, but I can't be sure, for he's shpakin' nothin' but his own avil lingo."

"Let him come in, then, if he's alone and isn't armed," replied Howell. And the Apache stalked gravely to the fire, and squatted beside it with a grunt of "How!" He was stripped to the breech-clout and moccasins, his lank, black hair confined by a strip of red flannel across the brows, and a buckskin "medicine-bag" suspended round his neck. The gleaming firelight revealed the most hideously brutal face that the lieutenant had ever seen. Jasaspi, the scout, wormed himself towards Howell noiselessly in the darkness.

"That's old Alchise!" he whispered, excitedly. "Ver' *maldito* bad Injun. He's got his warriors out in the *mesquite,* you bet. Thinks he's goin' wipe us out, or he wouldn't come in here. Ugh!"

Suddenly the visitor spoke. Pointing to the scout, he said: "Him 'terpreter?"

"*Si.* All right. *Bueno.* Go ahead; he'll interpret," replied Howell, and the chief plunged into his oration in a mixture of Apache and Spanish, translated by Jasaspi into a villanous compound of tongues which it would be maddening to reproduce.

"Says the Tinne *se fatigan del guerra.* Says they're tired of war; want peace. They ain't 'fraid *de los Americanos,* but they can't fight the scouts. Says he has a hundred warriors in the chaparral, and he wants to be friends. Liar! Wagh!" added Jasaspi on his own account, as the chief stopped talking.

"Very good," said Howell. "Tell him the sooner he gives himself up the better."

This was interpreted, and the ambassador replied:

"Says your words are good, and you are a big chief. Says his young men 'll want to kill us, but he won't let them. Wants us to give up our guns, so his young men won't be mad when they see us. Says he'll go with you to the Reserve, and you'll make a big talk to the agent, so that they'll get all their land back."

"Tell him that we won't give up our rifles, and that if he surrenders, I'll see that he's taken good care of till he's tried."

When this had been interpreted, the half-breed chief said no more, but after some seconds rose in silence and turned to go.

"No!" ejaculated Howell, sharply. "Sit down."

There were three separate clicks from the gloom, and the Apache, turning, saw three gaping muzzles covering his chest. He grunted, and after a moment of deliberation sullenly sat down again.

"Tie his feet, Clarke," said the lieutenant. "I'll fix his hands, and look out that he hasn't a knife."

But the Indian made no resistance beyond a series of half - articulate grunts. " Says his warriors 'll cut our hearts out and eat 'em if he's hurt," interpreted Jasaspi, grinning.

It was evidently time to light the signal. For this purpose a great pile of light wood had been collected about twenty feet from the enclosure, and Jasaspi undertook the perilous duty—perilous because it was almost certain that the dense scrub was lined with an unseen but vigilant enemy. He wriggled out along the ground, but as the first blue flame spluttered from the match there were twenty darting flashes from the cover, and a deafening rifle-volley. Bullets slapped viciously into the firewood, skipped over the stone rampart, and cut " r-r-rt " through the white tent-covers; but the fire had taken hold, and Jasaspi crawled back as he had gone, unwounded and triumphant. But the triumph was brief. Before one-quarter of the beacon was ignited the pile suddenly collapsed, and was flung in all directions by some unseen agency, but the yells of the savages showed that some of the number had simply crept up and scattered the fire. It lay strewn over the ground in scattered, flaming brands, but in face of the concealed rifles it would have been madness for one of the little party to attempt to reassemble it. It was evident that the Apaches, themselves clever signallers, were fully alive to the importance of preventing the besieged from sending any message.

After this misfortune there could be no possibility of signalling the column before sunrise, when the heliograph could be used, and the one necessity was to hold the post till that hour for the sake of the campaign, and as much longer as possible for the sake of their own lives.

The heavy firing did not last long, and presently only an occasional shot snapped out as an Apache fancied he saw a target over the low camp wall. The blazing brands had died out, and there was no moon, so that the battle-field was only half lighted by the great stars that cluster in the clear Arizona skies.

Between eleven and twelve o'clock the Apaches made an attempt, some twenty of them, to creep up to the wall and overpower the garrison at close quarters, but they were discovered and fired upon in the open ground. Two were shot as they lay, and the rest escaped to the chaparral under a heavy covering fire. Then, for a long time, hostilities lagged.

Every minute passed in quiet was a distinct gain to the Americans. The procession of the brilliant stars went over from east to west, and the night passed leaden-footed till it was that favorite hour for Indian attacks—that proverbially darkest hour which comes about three o'clock in the morning. The enemy's fire had almost entirely ceased, and this so disquieted the soldiers that one of the men cautiously kindled a brand at the fire and hurled it high over the rampart.

The brand blazed up as it flew through the air, and then fell into darkness, but the light had flashed for an instant upon crawling rifle-barrels and belts fitted with brass cartridge-heads. The discovery was greeted with shrill whoops and a rattling fire, and under this support the band of Apaches, which had already approached nearly to the camp, sprang up and endeavored to rush the defences. They were met by the muzzles of rifles and revolvers in the hands of men who worked them with the regularity of machinery. No sooner did a warrior appear at the rampart than he was shot down. But the whites themselves were not without loss. The Americans fought in silence for the most part, but the high-pitched, barking yelps of the Apaches dominated the uproar.

The shots diminished of a sudden, there was not a glimpse of the enemy, and the soldiers found themselves with nothing to shoot at but the occasional flashes from the thicket. The attack was repulsed.

Some shooting was kept up by the concealed enemy, but it was with less spirit. Howell took the covers from the heliographic mirrors and adjusted the tripods, ready for the first beam of sunlight.

It was yet fifteen minutes, which seemed fifteen months, before the first segment of the sun appeared above the straight eastern sky-line. A golden ray played over the grim scene of the battle-field, and the lieutenant sprang up and placed his tripods in position, partly behind the tent, which in some degree screened him from the eyes of the Apache marksmen.

There was bright sunlight on the butte almost instantly. Directly in front, six feet away, the great precipice dropped sheer, and away thirty miles to the left rose the hilltop where the second signal-station was placed. The lieutenant focussed the light from the receiver upon the signalling-mirror, then sighted

the crossed hairs in the telescope upon the hilltop, and directed the ray full upon the distant
station—the calling-up signal. Almost immediately were seen two rapid, fiery dots in the
distance, indicating: " Understood. Go on."

" Dot, dash; dot, dash, dash, dot; dot, dash;
dash, dot, dash, dot," signalled Howell, his
finger on the shifting - key, while the bullets
zipped around him. "Apaches attacking post
in force all night. Have captured Alchise,
and—"

There was a surprising interruption. The
captured Apache had, as it transpired later,
been chewing industriously at his bonds all
through the hours of darkness, and had got
them completely severed. Now, as if he had
heard his name called, he sprang up with a
startling whoop, and made a dash for liberty.
Jasaspi was up and after him like a flash, pulling at his pistol, which he wore in an open
holster, plains fashion, when a volley blazed
out from the bush. The scout stopped short,
made two drunken steps, and dropped, while
Alchise whirled about on his heel and collapsed
limply across the stone-built rampart.

There was no more shooting from the enemy.
Probably the hostiles recognized immediately

that they had unwittingly slain their chief, and a chief is prized by the renegade Apaches, who depend upon him for moral support. The besiegers melted away, and in half an hour they had vanished completely.

But Alchise was not dead, after all. He recovered consciousness in a few minutes, and the soldiers dragged him back. They bandaged him up and gave him what relief they could, for he was wanted alive rather than dead.

That was practically the end of the campaign. The *ranchesia* had been captured on the night before, and the remaining hostiles were hunted through the cañons and deserts till they surrendered. Lieutenant Howell's plucky stand really brought about most of this success, but he never got any official credit for it, because heroism was commonplace among officers in the old days of the West. Most of the hostiles were allowed to go back to the reserve without further punishment, but Alchise was tried on a variety of counts after his recovery, and sentenced to twenty years in prison at Prescott, Arizona.

6

"BILLY" OF BATTERY B

The Story of " A Horse as was a Horse "

I

IT was in the hush of those quiet hours after " stables," when the golden sunshine fell aslant through the skylight over the rows of stalls, when the oats were finished, and the only sound was the rustle of sweet-smelling hay — from which the dust floated upward into the yellow block of light above and filled it with dancing motes—that Billy and Bob had their most confidential chats. It was then that Billy had pointed out to him the pitfalls and snares that beset every young high-tempered horse in the service, and was clearly shown the error of his way; and it was then that he poured into the ears of Bob, that hardened old campaigner,

all the yearnings and ambitions of his imma-
ture colthood.

All day long a white-haired old major-general, who had led his corps through the Wilder-
ness, sat his horse on top of a hill, and watched
cavalry charge solid lines of infantry in the
teeth of mowing magazine fire, and infantry, ·
in their turn, walk calmly up to the belching
muzzles of a battery's guns. There was a very
weary look on the old general's face, for it
was one of those days they call "field-days,"
when, according to the instructions issued on
little slips of white and brown paper, "the
conditions of actual warfare are to be simu-
lated as far as possible," and all the simula-
tion results in is noisy bawling of orders, dust,
smoke, and recrimination and disgust on the
part of officers, men, and horses. At one time,
however, the general's face wore a pleasant
smile—that was when B Battery, enveloped
in a seething cloud of dust, rolled over the
plain hither and thither, vomiting forth flame
and smoke, like some mighty leviathan warring
the elements. Then the general had smiled,
keeping his eyes on the stop-watch ticking in
his hand, and listening to the cadenced de-
tonations of the six Hotchkiss pieces as they

swung "into battery," right, left, front, and rear.

By and by, when all the roar and confusion were over, and the battery had come home, tired, smoke-begrimed, and dusty, with their heads drooping and the reds of the choked nostrils quivering, Billy tried to founder himself by drinking a bucket of water some one had carelessly left in the corral, and Bob the wise had dragged him away from it and gently kicked him.

It had been a momentous day for Billy. He had been promoted from off-swing horse, No. 1 gun, to near wheeler, same piece — Bob, the regular near-wheel horse, having a sore back. For the first time in his military career he had felt a driver's knees pressing his sides, and the responsibility that all this involved had been very great. Then half the time the lead and the swing teams stood loose in their traces, so that Billy and Bob had to start the limber unassisted. Between this and the responsibility and the uneven ground, with the limber tongue flying up and threatening to break his driver's legs and Billy's ribs, Billy felt his lot was not one to be envied.

He had seen the sorrels of the cavalry troop

next door sweep over the plain on a sabre charge like a whirlwind, and pulling at the near-wheel trace of No. 1 gun seemed very tame work compared to a free, wild run like theirs over the green bottom. It set Billy thinking of the old blue-grass farm where he was foaled, with its long stretches of meadow that he used to scamper and frolic over in his coltish baby days. Then he leaned over and rubbed his nose along Bob's neck very deferentially, and said, softly:

"Haven't you ever longed to be out of your collar and charge like the cavalry, Bob—just to lay yourself out flat on the green grass and go on till you burst?"

Bob stopped tossing up his hay, and looked with a dignified expression of pity at Billy.

"My dear colt! Where are your thoughts wandering? We of Battery B are superior to all that sort of thing. That's all very well for a harumscarum lot like those sorrels over the fence, who stampede at a red rag when they are herded out, and who would scatter over forty miles of country if you fired a blank from our three 2-inch among 'em. But for us, Billy, our position in the service does not permit of such pranks. And as for charging, real charging, what charge ever equalled the charge of Senarmont's ten light batteries on the Russian centre at Friedland? They unlimbered 120 yards from the front.* Why, cavalry ain't in it with us, Billy!"

To this wise answer, Billy was unable to reply; but, nevertheless, deep down in his soul was a longing for a frolic on the old blue-grass meadow, and a half - formed wish for a stampede of the battery herd—a thing that never happened.

They were all slashing big bays, the horses of Battery B, and even for horses of a crack light battery they were a proud and exclusive lot. The service forgives the artillery, in a measure, for their assumption of superior importance, but so patronizing were those battery horses to the sorrels of the cavalry troop in the adjacent yard — whom they regarded as removed only one degree from quartermaster's mules—that the sorrels approached even the battery fence with awe and trepidation.

" There are whole lots of things you don't know yet, Billy," said the sage of the battery herd, nosing over into his mate's manger for

* Report of Marshal Victor, Commander-in-Chief First Corps.

a wisp of hay. "Your homesickness for that sleepy old farm back in Kentucky makes me tired. Instead of having the glorious mission of hauling Uncle Sam's cannon into battle, you'd rather be hauling potatoes into market for some lanky old farmer. But if you had seen what I've seen, and heard what I've heard, you'd feel thankful for your destiny. Why, colt, I've met fellows that dragged their guns up Cemetery Ridge and Little Round Top, and saw them stop Pickett's charge at the high-water mark of the Confederacy! Those fellows saved their country, Billy. You've a mission, colt—a mission! And you want to get all those crazy ideas about free runs on the old farm and foolish cavalry charges out of your head. It's lucky for you that you weighed 1500 instead of 1100, and didn't have skinny withers, or you'd never have the distinction of belonging to Battery B. You'd have gone to the cavalry, and in four years the inspector would have condemned you and sold you into an ash-cart.

"It's not in bran mashes and big feeds of corn that the joys of life lie; it's in appreciating your mission and making the most of it. We are the bowels of the army, the army is the blood and body of the government, and our government is the hope of the world. That's what my father used to say to me, and he saw the whole thing demonstrated in the rebellion. Now what you want to do is to study your job. When you are flying around out there on the parade, remember that the life of your rider and the cannoneers behind you, and, in battle, often the result of the day, depend on your keeping your feet. In 'action front,' when you leave the piece, throw yourself into your collar like a cannon ball, or you'll get pulled over some time, and, above all, keep your eyes on the ground so you can jump the hollows and the limber tongue won't fly up and break your rider's legs. If you do that, and always have your tugs taut, you will get your reward some day, though we ain't generally mentioned in histories, Billy."

"It is all very well for you to talk like that, Bob," said Billy. "You are satisfied and proud of your position, but if your old home had been one like the one I left back East, you would feel differently. There were no potatoes to haul and no lanky old farmer there. My sire won the blue ribbon on Churchill Downs,' and my master was a real, old Kentucky gentleman. I could not have been better treated if I had been the favorite of an Arab chief. We bred racing stock. Of course, I was only a half-breed, and too heavy to race, so I stayed quietly at home. Then master's daughter took a fancy to me in my puppy days, and made me her pet. Every morning she came tripping out to see me in the paddock with an apple or a lump of sugar and a caress. She was the only one that ever rode me, and her bridle hand was so light and her seat so firm and gentle that it was a joy to have her on one's back. We were all very happy back there in those days, Bob, except master, who was always worried and sad. You see, the prices of horses had been sinking lower every year, and the mortgage on the farm was eating everything away, and master saw the day staring him in the face when all he had would have to be sold to pay it. The day came, sure enough, with the sheriff and the red auction flag, along with the throngs of curious, callous, hard-featured people. There were some white faces in the family, but not a word of complaint from master's wife and daughter, who went about calm and composed, with a brave smile on their faces, though their eyes were very soft and shiny with sympathy for heartbroken master.

" One by one the dear old things they loved —the pictures, the books, the time - blackened mahogany furniture — were carted away in wagons. Then it came our turn in the stables, and we were walked out and handled and punched by veterinaries. We were trotted around the yard. Our pedigrees were read, and all kinds of lies told about us before the auctioneer knocked us down to the highest bidder. After it was all over, and I was tied up to a horse-dealer's wagon out in the road, very blue and brokenhearted over our misfortunes, I felt a pair of soft arms steal around my neck, and my little girl's cheek nestling close to me. There was no one near us, and she had come to say good-bye. When I turned and rubbed my nose on her shoulder she was crying softly.

" ' Good-bye, you dear, old Billy,' she whispered. ' Good-bye! Always be your good and kind and gentle and true self.'

" I know I'll never meet anybody, Bob, who will love me as she did, and now do you wonder that I keep thinking of that old blue-grass farm way back in Kentucky ?"

Bob blinked sympathetically, and rubbed his nose up and down Billy's neck to cheer him.

" At the same time, colt," said he, soberly,

" don't you think that little girl would be happier if she knew you were following her advice ?"

It was very late in the stables now; most of the battery horses were down asleep in their beds of hay. When the sad, resonant notes of " taps " came floating in on the night air, poor, tired Billy did not hear them, for he was fast asleep, too, and dreaming of long vistas of blue-grass meadow, and the gentle voice and hand that used to guide and cheer him on his way.

II

The drifting snow, dry and biting as salt, was filling all the hollows and crannies around a desolate camp at the Rosebud Agency, on the flat, brown plateau of South Dakota, one cheerless December afternoon in 1890. Inside the dreary Sibley tents the men were huddled together under blankets, trying to thaw out, and discussing the probable outcome of the uprising of the Sioux ghost-dancers, whose threatening actions had brought all the available horse and foot of our army to the cold, barren region where they lived.

A man had arisen among them who called himself "the Messiah." He had talked to them in a frenzied and impassioned way in a strain that is ever welcome in the young Indian's ears—of war and the glory of revenge; of the fancied and real wrongs they had suffered at the white man's hands; of the cheating and stealing of the White Father's agents. Then straightway they had streaked their faces with hideous dashes of yellow, vermilion, and blue, and stalked into the agency full of an unholy desire for slaughter, which had found expression in the saying of a big chief who proclaimed "he could not die happy until he had eaten a white man's heart."

The word of the government had gone forth, for fifteen thousand rabid Indians cannot be dealt with tenderly, and the telegraph wires were kept smoking with hurrying messages to troops who were coming helter-skelter from north, south, east, and west. From each side of the square two hundred miles of desert, large bodies of troops were drawing in on the reservation, while back and forth over their bleak land a restless wave of Indians swept, seeking to avoid the inevitable contingency of surrender or annihilation.

The government was trying very hard to bring the Sioux to reason with a great show of force, and the older and wiser heads among the Indians were seconding their efforts to prevent a fruitless shedding of blood. But these efforts had been made too late, for the fever of war was in the hot blood of the young Sioux braves. Already there had been killing done, and new-made graves studded the fast-whitening winter prairie. Sitting Bull had been shot while resisting arrest, and his followers were mad with desire for revenge, while the government had decreed a general disarming of the Sioux.

Down at the end of the agency camp was a small detachment from Battery B—two guns and fifteen men, and picketed near by in the chill of the storm, shivering under their canvas covers, were Billy and Bob, with about a dozen of the battery bays.

"Wot's ther use of our bloomin' guns out 'ere, I'd like ter know?" said Driver Burke to his comrades in the snow-bound tent. "Chasin' Injians with cannon is the wust tomfoolishness I ever 'eard of." But we must judge Driver Burke leniently, for when a soldier is quartered out on a frozen prairie in what seems to him a purposeless way, all things look foolish.

Then up piped a pallid recruit from under a pile of blankets. "Now that they got th' hull outfit of 'em surrounded, they ought ter let us go 'ome an' get warm—sure." This brought a smile to the seared, weather-beaten face of the old sergeant in charge, who was smoking his pipe, and refusing to allow himself to be otherwise than cheerful and contented.

"If you fellers would stop studyin' the conduk of the campaign an' the akshuns of the commanding officer, you'd be better off," interrupted the sergeant. "You ain't gettin' thirteen dollars a month for ter advise the major-gen'ral. All you got ter do is ter obey orders and' keep your faces closed, an' I think if you go out an' hustle up a pile of wood for ternight, you'd feel better."

While that conversation was going on inside of Battery B's tent, down at headquarters the major-general was listening to the broken, impetuous story of a pale, half-frozen orderly with a bloody bandage tied around his head.

The message was short and very pressing. When the soldier finished he was dismissed, and the grave, careworn general turned and asked his aid if there were any mounted troops in camp.

"No, sir," was the answer. "The cavalry is all out, but there is that battery detachment."

The general thought of the fifteen long miles between the camp and place where succor was needed so badly, of the trail heavy with snow, and he sighed for the absent cavalry. Then he thought of the quiet, grim lieutenant of B Battery, who had been chafing at the useless rôle he had been forced to play in the campaign, and had repeatedly solicited permission to show what his little Hotchkiss guns could do in settling matters with the Sioux, and he remembered the slashing big bay horses that the battery was so proud of.

"Send for Lieutenant Dacre, captain," was his order to the silent aide.

When the battery commander received the message he ran hot-footed to headquarters, in glad anticipation of work to do, and his first look at the stern, anxious face of his chief told him what it was.

"The —th are having a row with Big Foot's band down on Wounded Knee Creek. They need help badly, and I have nothing here that could reach them soon enough. Do you think you can get your guns there in time to be of any use? It's fifteen miles over the ridge west."

"I should like to try, general."

"Very good. Go ahead. We will be several hours behind with the infantry."

There was a scramble around the battery tent a few minutes later, and a rush of men laden with harness and accoutrements over to the horses at the picket-line. Never before did the battery drivers hitch so quickly, and the cannoneers ran the guns and limbers out of the canvas sheds with an agility that on-lookers had never seen equalled. No bugles were blown, no orders were given; there was no need to tell anybody to make haste, for the orderly with the bloody bandage around his head had staggered down the camp street on his way to the hospital with a horror - stricken face, telling every one that the Custer massacre was being repeated down at Wounded Knee, and that the "Fighting —th" were making another hopeless struggle against their old, pitiless enemies.

Out of sight of the bewildered infantry soldiers emerging from their tents the battery whirled, soon lost to view in the swirling snow.

There was no time for a God-speed you or a farewell cheer. Cannoneers and drivers stared grimly ahead, and only one thought was in their heads—to get there in time, which depended altogether on the horses.

Did those horses hear what the general had told the battery commander, or had they seen the wounded orderly reeling through the camp to the hospital? That is not given us to know. At any rate, Billy and Bob knew that their battery was on business of a most urgent nature, or they would never be flying at racing speed over the cold, snowy plain towards the distant hills and the sinking sun. They could almost measure the importance of their task by the way the drivers on the swings and leads laid the quirt over their teams; but the wheelers on No. 1 gun did not need any urging.

"Run low and steady, Billy; quit jerking your collar. We have a long, hard run to make, and who knows what might happen if we don't made it? They need us badly somewhere—a regiment must be getting slaughtered."

"Were you ever in action, Bob? How does it feel?" asked Billy, as they bowled along.

"Oh, you feel as jolly as can be. It's all kinds of fun. Everybody goes clean crazy, except us. Some of 'em laugh, and some of 'em cry; some of 'em, in fact, most of 'em, first time, get very sick. Men are so much more foolish than we are about these things. Look out! Slide, Billy, slide!"

Just then they came to some ice holes. The off leader slipped and fell, bringing down his mate; on top of the leads tumbled, crashing, the swing team, while Billy and Bob just managed to keep out of the awful mess by sitting down on their rumps and sliding on their tails. They dragged out of the squirming wreck the driver of the lead with his skull cracked, and the driver of the swings unconscious and bleeding, and laid them tenderly down on the snow while the horses were looked to.

" Two of 'em 's bruk ther legs, lieutenant," sang out the sergeant, " an' this 'ere swing horse is stove up inside."

" Take three horses off No. 2, and put them in their places. Stay behind with 2, sergeant, take those wounded men, and follow us as fast as you can," said the lieutenant.

So in a few seconds No. 1 was rolling ahead again, leaving behind its crippled mate and two limp, unconscious forms stretched out on its limber. On the foaming horses sped.

86

"My soul! What a narrow shave that was for us, Bob!"

"Never you mind thinking about narrow escapes," answered Bob; "you just keep your eyes on the ground, and jump those ice holes. Don't forget to sit down and slide if anybody goes down in front. There is one thing sure, we have to get this gun somewhere in very short order, or a regiment will be slaughtered; it must be a regiment, for they wouldn't move us like this for anything less."

Of a truth, the words of old Bob were timely and to the point. Over the snow-covered prairie frozen hummocks were scattered here and there, and around these wicked little lumps were rings of steely, black ice—ice that sometimes broke and lacerated ankle-joints fearfully, while sometimes the rough-shod hoofs slipped over like skates.

They were half-way up the gentle grade that led to the gap in the ridge to the west, but they never shortened their long, free stride. Men and horses settled down to the work with that grim determination that wins out many a forlorn hope. Not a sound, not a message from the desperate fight beyond, had reached them yet. The lieutenant was riding ahead of the

careening gun, picking out the trail. All at
once there loomed up against the sky-line of
the ridge ahead a big six-mule ambulance,
which came tearing down the grade to them.
It was full of shrieking, wounded men. The
lieutenant pulled back to speak to them. There
were men with the madness of the fight on
them yet, cursing the doctors who had taken
them away; sad dying men with blue faces,
and pallid, sunny-haired boys with tears running down their cheeks—all of them crazy,
irrational, incoherent.

"Push on! Push on, or there will be nobody
left over there," was all the ambulance driver
could say when questioned. And that gun did
push on as hard as strength of man and beast
could push.

Up at the entrance of the gap there was
something waiting for Battery B—something
that men and horses did not expect. It was
an ambush that the crafty enemy had planned
to cut off the longed-for relief. With wily
cunning they had let the ambulance pass them
unmolested. Invisible things were hiding behind crag and bowlder—things with dark, un-
human faces, scanning with their gleaming
eyes every detail of the little gun detachment

which was climbing confidently up to the steep, narrow gap beneath them, waiting patiently till even the element of skill was not needed to make murder complete. Then the signal was given, the volley was fired, and men and horses fell. Both the lead and swing teams and the lieutenant's horse were shot dead in their tracks. Billy saw old Bob quiver, sink, and straighten himself with an effort, he also felt his fore-leg give way as a burning pain shot across his ankle. All this time from the rocks above the Winchesters of the Indians were spitting white puffs of smoke downward, and bullets were singing below and above, in front and rear. The men were all killed at the first fire, except the lieutenant and two drivers, and they were busy hacking away with their sabres at the traces of the dead leaders and swings. In a moment the gun was freed of its dead horses, and Billy and Bob found themselves pulling it up through the gap all alone —one horse on three legs, for the fourth had been disabled by a shot, and the other with a bullet in his lungs. Still, they struggled and strained every aching fibre, and the gun went up the gap.

What a great, noble soul can do in the hour

of agony and need—till nature calls a halt—is a marvel to the world.

Just as they pulled out of range of the ambush Bob fell dying in the snow, and as he looked up at Billy with the mournful eyes of one who dies while his task is yet undone, I think he must have said: " You do it for me, Billy!"

They cut Bob loose, and the lieutenant and the two men put their shoulders to the limber and started the piece uphill once more. Four hundred yards up the terrible grade Billy pulled that gun for them, at every step digging his wounded off front leg into the sharp shale and jagged ice of the mountain trail; but his agony and pain were nearly over. At the brow of the divide they looked down into the valley where the fight was going on.

Below them a thin blue skirmish-line, stretched out in a crescent, was replying feebly to the rapid and destructive fire of the Indians, sheltered in their village and in the commanding ground on the other side. There were many silent gaps in the blue skirmish-line, and the ground between it and the Indians was scattered with rigid blue-clad forms and the stiff, tawny figures of dead Sioux.

90

If the authors of the " Drill Regulations for Light Artillery " could have seen that gun, drawn by a horse on three legs, and manned by an officer and two privates, go " into battery " on the brow of that hill, they would have marvelled greatly.

The limber did not come around on a gallop, by a left traverse—as the book says it should —but the gun was in position just as quickly as if it had; for two men had drawn the pin and uncoupled the tailpiece from the limber before they halted. They ran the gun out " by hand " to the brink, while the lieutenant—self-instituted powder-monkey—dug deep into the limber chest and filled his arms full of long, slim shrapnel shells.

Billy, tottering on three legs behind them, saw everything—the breech opened, the cartridge pushed home, and the breech closed and locked. He saw the lieutenant down on his knees adjusting the sights, and pointing the piece which exact nicety at a swarm of Sioux behind the tepees in the village.

Driver Burke stood with his knees bent and the lanyard taut in his hand, impatient for the word. In a low, firm tone it came, " Fire!" A long tongue of flame shot forth, then a blast of white, cloudy smoke, and, after a distinct pause, the sharp detonation rang out and deafened them. Straining forward, they saw the shell burst over the village, and tepees, blankets, ponies, and Indians seemed to be struck by a tornado. Then they sent shell after shell shrieking over the valley into the village and the Indian position. The hissing wail of the twisting shrapnel as they flew through the air had a most terrifying effect on the Sioux. They thought they heard the voices of the dead they had killed and tortured crying for vengeance.

As if hurried on by the ghosts of the departed, swiftly and silently every Indian fled, and nothing was left below to fire at but a mass of whirling wreckage.

Cheer on cheer came ringing up from the rescued regiment below, but the lieutenant and the two exhausted men lying flat on the ground by the side of the reeking gun did not hear them. Their eyes were fastened on a gaunt, haggard horse swaying to and fro on three legs, his soft, pleading eyes swimming with pain.

A look flashed on the lieutenant's face that made his hard features tender and womanly.

Then it was that Driver Burke, the worst black-guard in the battery, spoke his mind.

"That's a horse as is a horse, an 'e ought ter 'ave a medal as big as ther moon."

The lieutenant looked at Driver Burke, and a bond of sympathy was established between them right there and then. The other man was dumb as an oyster, but he never took his staring, wet eyes off Billy.

"Ther' ain't no such thing as givin' a horse a wooden leg," said Burke, meditatively; "an' the kindest thing we can do is ter do our duty." And they did.

According to Burke, Billy's shiny, brown eyes thanked him as he fired.

"If there is any horse's heaven," says Burke, "where they does nothin' but play on ther blue-grass meadows among the daisies all day long—you'll find Billy there."

They all received medals of honor, every member of that gun detachment; but among themselves they often say that, "he who most deserved a medal never received one"—meaning, of course, Billy of Battery B.

FLORIDE'S PATIENT

A True Story of the Civil War

A GREAT battle was fought near Floride's home in the South. All day long she listened to the distant roar of the cannon. She had not a very clear idea of what the quarrel was all about, but she was an ardent little rebel, nevertheless.

She hated the Yankees bitterly when she heard that they had gained the victory, and left hundreds of Southern soldiers wounded and dead on the field, and she grieved over the thought of their suffering until it seemed as if she must do something to help them. The dear, old church where she used to go to Sunday-school had been turned into a hospital. Floride would often wander near it, thinking of all the pain and misery within, until one day she peeped through the open door. Inside she saw rows of narrow cots, with haggard-looking men stretched upon them. Other men, evidently surgeons and nurses, were hurrying back and forth in a way that seemed to Floride noisy and heartless. Just opposite the door lay a boy, with dark, damp hair, and such a sad, tired face that Floride could not keep back tears of pity.

Frank Laine had closed his eyes to shut out the dreadful sight of so much suffering, and his mind had wandered home again. Oh, if his mother were only here to put her cool hand on his burning head for one minute, or his little sister, just to say she was sorry for him! But there was no one to pity him now, and they would never know how he longed for them.

He opened his eyes wearily, and saw standing in a gleam of sunshine that fell across the doorway a little white-robed figure with shining hair, and he wondered vaguely if it was an angel as it came slowly towards him.

"Do you want some?" Floride whispered; and without waiting for an answer she flung her bunch of wild flowers on the cot and ran away.

Then Frank knew it was no angel, but a tender-hearted little girl like his own sister

Margaret, and an overwhelming rush of homesickness made him burst into tears. Poor fellow! he was no hero now, though he had fancied himself one not long ago when he ran
away, from home to join the Northern army.
He had meant to write to his mother after the
first battle, and tell of his wonderful deeds of
bravery and the praise he had gained. But
there was nothing of the kind to tell. Heroes
are not left lying on the roadside for hours,
dizzy with pain, while the army sweeps by and
wins the victory without their help. He would
never write home now. Everything had turned
out as his father foretold, and he could never,
never expect to earn forgiveness.

He hoped Floride would come again. She
was like a little bit of home unexpectedly find-
ing its way into the dreary place. The night
did not seem so long and tedious when he was
thinking about her, wondering whether she
was a rebel, and where she lived, and whether
she would come to-morrow. He was so anxious
to see her again that he grew restless and fever-
ish as the time wore on, but the nurses were
too busy to notice him. There were many
others of more importance in their eyes than
the drummer - boy, who was so dangerously

wounded that he probably never would get well.

To his delight the golden head peeped in about nine o'clock, and after a moment's hesitation Floride walked over to the cot.

"See, I've brought you something," she whispered, her cheeks pink with suppressed excitement; and she produced from under her apron a china mug full of milk. Such a thing was unknown in the hospital, and Frank was always thirsty.

"That's good!" he cried, draining it eagerly. "That's like home. It makes me think of Dapple. Dapple was my cow, you know."

"Oh, have you got a cow?" asked Floride.

"I used to have. She was fine, I tell you. Whenever I came in sight she'd run up to me and lay her head on my shoulder, and— Oh, well," he broke off, hastily, as he felt a lump rising in his throat, "there's no use talking about it. I'll never see her again."

"Did the Yankees steal her?" demanded Floride. "The wicked, cruel, horrid things!"

"See here, you mustn't talk like that!" exclaimed Frank. "I'm a Yankee myself."

"Why, I thought you were nice!" cried Floride. "I thought you were a Confederate.

I'm sorry I brought you the milk. I hate you! You killed my Uncle Paul. Oh, you bad, bad man!" And with a stamp of her foot she ran away.

In vain Frank called her back. He had no quarrel with *her,* little rebel though she was, and he felt lonelier than ever when she was gone.

Poor Floride went home and had a good cry. Down in the bottom of her heart she had always thought of Yankees as black men who ate little children. It was a great disappointment to find out her mistake, and, besides, she was really very sorry for the wounded soldier; but she resolved never to go to the hospital again, or take the "Yank" things to eat. If she could only have had a long talk with her mother about him! But Mrs. Elmer was many miles away, and somehow Floride could not tell her secrets to Aunt Carrie. Nothing would make her believe that any Yankee was nice, and she would be glad Frank was wounded.

The next day was Sunday, and in the afternoon Floride went off to Sunday-school with her heart full of "hatred, malice, and all uncharitableness." The Yankees had taken away their church, and they had to meet in Miss

Nelson's house. That was another reason for hating them. Besides, hadn't the "Yanks" killed dear Uncle Paul, whom Miss Nelson had promised to marry?

The text that day was "Love your enemies." It made Floride feel uncomfortable, for just as she said it, it struck her that the Yankees were her enemies. Miss Nelson did not say one word about the Northern soldiers, but she reminded the girls of what bitter foes our dear Lord had, and how He prayed, "Father, forgive them, for they know not what they do," and she told them that each and all must try to follow His example, and do good to those that hated them. Suddenly she stopped, and bursting into tears, said: "Go home, children, go home."

"Well, I don't care what Miss Nelson says, I hate the Yankees!" exclaimed one of the older girls, as they went slowly out; and the others cried out, "Oh, of course, Miss Nelson couldn't mean to love Yankees!"

But Floride was silent. She knew very well that Miss Nelson *had* meant the Northern soldiers, and she resolved to forgive the wounded drummer-boy, and see what she could do to make him happier.

Frank had watched for her all day, but when evening came he gave up and tried not to be disappointed, but it was very hard to be brave. He had had no supper. How could he eat the coarse, hastily cooked hospital food? He was not hungry, but he was terribly thirsty. His head ached, too. The pain seemed to vanish when a light footstep that certainly was not that of one of the surgeons fell on his ear, and Floride came softly in, looking a little frightened.

"Here," she whispered, "I brought you some more milk and some jelly, and I'm sorry I called you a Yankee. Good-bye!"

"Oh, stop, little girl, stop!" said the "Yankee," eagerly. "You needn't be sorry. I don't mind; and thank you for the things. Won't you stay and talk? I'm so— It's kind of lonely here."

"I should think it would be," said Floride, sympathetically; "but I can't stay now. It's almost dark. I'll come again to-morrow, right after breakfast," and with a happy nod she flew away.

The next day, and every day after for more than a week, she visited her patient faithfully. She always brought something nice for him to eat or drink, and Frank never dreamed that she was denying herself to give it to him. Her visits were the one bright spot in days that were cloudy with pain.

The other patients watched for her, too, and were better for the sight of her sunny face; while the doctors, when they thought of her at all, concluded that she did the wounded boy good, and they made no objection to her presence. As for Frank, he was contented to lie still, with closed eyes, while she chattered to him, or murmured softly the hymns she knew, if he was in great pain. " There is a green hill far away," and " Once in royal David's city," were his favorites.

Sometimes, when he felt better than usual, he would tell her about the dear Connecticut farm, and just how his mother looked, and how stern his father sometimes was, and yet how kind.

Floride would beg him to write to them and say he was sorry for his disobedience, and tell them he was wounded, but Frank always shut his lips in a decided way and shook his head at this. He was very proud, poor boy! One day he asked Floride to bring him a sheet of paper and an envelope.

"Are you going to write to your mother?" asked Floride, eagerly.

"Yes, but I am not going to send it now," Frank answered. "I want you to take care of it for me, and afterwards—when I—die—I want you to send it."

That Frank was going to die was a new idea to Floride. She gazed at him wistfully while the tears rolled down her cheeks, and could not speak; but when he smiled back at her bravely, and said, "Oh, don't cry! It doesn't matter much," with a great sob, she rushed out into the woods, and throwing herself down on the grass, cried as if her heart would break.

It was a very short letter that the poor boy wrote, for his strength was failing fast. He told how good the little rebel had been to him, and how she had promised to send the letter after he was dead, so that they might know he longed for their forgiveness, and missed them every minute night and day. Then he gave it to Floride, and they never spoke of the subject again, but whenever the little girl entered the hospital after that she trembled for fear they would tell her that Frank was dead.

Miss Elmer had so much to do, and so many things to occupy her mind in those dark days of the war, that she did not think a great deal about the comings and goings of her little niece. Not long after this, however, she said to Miss Nelson: "I don't know what to make of Floride. She is the strangest child—"

"Why, what has she been doing now?" asked Miss Nelson.

"Oh, nothing; but she has such queer ideas. She has taken a fancy to eat all her dainties in private. She never will drink her milk at table now, and she is always begging for jelly, or berries, or something else to eat. Such an appetite cannot be healthy."

"Well, let her enjoy herself if she can," said Miss Nelson. "I suppose she likes to go off to the woods and play tea-party."

"Poor child, she little realizes what terrible suffering is at our door!"

But Miss Elmer found out that day how much of the suffering Floride did realize, when one of the Northern surgeons brought the little girl home in his arms white and faint. A man had had his leg cut off in the hospital, he explained, and no one had known that Floride was there until they heard a low groan, and she fell fainting to the floor. They had

103

revived her, and the surgeon had undertaken to bring her home and explain matters.

Floride only half understood what he was saying. She knew her aunt was puzzled and angry, but the room seemed to be spinning round, and she felt as if she did not care a great deal what happened when she heard the surgeon say: "It's doubtful if he pulls through."

"Oh, don't let him die!" she cried, springing up with sudden strength. "Oh, Aunt Carrie, poor Frank mustn't die! Oh, please, dear God, don't let him die!"

But all Aunt Carrie answered was: "Floride, I am surprised!" Then she turned to the surgeon with lofty courtesy and said: "Thank you for your kindness. Floride shall not trouble you again."

"You must not keep her away," he answered, pleasantly. "She does young Laine a world of good. If anything will help him out, it is the way she takes care of him. Good-bye, little nurse," he added, and was off.

In vain Floride begged and pleaded to be allowed to see Frank once more, in vain she explained that she was only trying to love her enemies, in vain she declared that Frank would die if she did not go. The only thing Miss Elmer would say on the subject was to repeat, coldly: "Floride, I am surprised!"

Floride was very lonely and unhappy after that. She wondered sadly whether Frank would think she had forgotten him, and whether he really would die all alone in that dreadful hospital. Suddenly a happy thought seized her, and she acted on it immediately. She would send the letter he had written to his mother, inclosed in a note of her own. Over this she took great pains.

"Dear Mrs. Laine," she wrote, "Frank is not dead. If you could come and nurse him, perhaps he would get well. I hope you will forgive him. He is a good boy.
"Your loving   FLORIDE."

The days that followed were full of suspense. She had no doubt that Frank's mother would come, but she was afraid Frank would be angry with her. She had promised to keep the letter until he died, and now she had broken her promise. What would he think of her?

One day she was having a cry all by herself in the summer-house when she saw Miss Nelson come up the garden walk. Dear, kind Miss

Nelson! At any other time Floride would have run to meet her, but she was too utterly wretched now to want to see anybody.

Miss Nelson stayed a long time, and Floride sat listlessly in the summer-house, wondering what they were talking about, but seeming to see through all her dreamy thoughts Frank's tired, patient eyes watching for her.

By and by Miss Nelson came out with Miss Elmer. As they went slowly down the walk, Floride heard her Sunday-school teacher say: "Now you will let her go, won't you, Carrie dear?"

"A Yankee soldier," Miss Elmer said, in feeble remonstrance. She hated the North bitterly, but she could not look into Miss Nelson's sweet, sad face, remembering how much she had suffered by that cruel war, and yet steel her heart against the wounded soldier for whom her friend was pleading.

"He will never fight again, poor fellow," said Miss Nelson, softly. "She did him so much good, and since she ceased to come he has just pined away."

"Well," said Aunt Carrie, reluctantly, and out of the summer-house flew Floride.

"Oh, let me go now, please—this minute!"

106

she begged. "Please, please, please do, Aunt Carrie."

Now, Miss Elmer never did anything by halves. "Well," she said again, but assentingly this time. "And if you will go, I might as well send the boy something to eat. Can you wait until I pack the basket?"

"Yes; oh yes!" chirped Floride; but she was sorry she had consented after a while, for it took Aunt Carrie so long. Too happy to sit still, she flew about picking flowers for her soldier, and when at last the basket was filled with all sorts of dainties to tempt a sick man's appetite, she rushed off.

Over sticks and stones she flew, taking the short-cut through the woods in her hot haste, and at every step out flew something from the basket. Peaches rolled under the trees, a little stream of milk trickled down the front of her new frock, and cookies strewed her pathway, but she was perfectly unconscious of the havoc. There was the dear church at last, and there was Frank. But oh, how changed! She had thought he was thin and pale before, but now his eyes were sunken, and there were dark circles around them, and his blue lips made a hard line that told of pain even to the child.

"Oh, Frank! Frank!" she moaned, and he held out his arms and clasped her close to him.

"Don't go away, Florrie," he murmured. "I haven't anybody but you."

"Auntie wouldn't let me come before," she whispered, sinking her voice involuntarily because his was so feeble.

"I know," he answered. "But I was sure she'd let you come before—I died."

"Oh, Frank, you mustn't!" moaned the little girl.

"I'm not afraid. If mamma was here, perhaps, I would be. But I don't mind if I do, now I've got you again."

His mention of his mother reminded Floride of the confession she had to make, and set her heart beating wildly. She felt as if she could not tell him at once, so to change the subject she said: "I reckon Aunt Carrie is sorry she wouldn't let me come. She sent a whole lot of things for you to eat. See!" and she triumphantly took off the basket cover.

Behold, the only thing the basket contained was a broken cup! Frank actually smiled at the child's rueful face. "Never mind," he said; "I don't want to eat, Floride; I just want to look at you. I'm not half so homesick now you are here."

"Are you yet homesick?" asked Floride, eagerly.

"Oh, *don't!*" groaned Frank.

"My darling! My precious boy!" cried a voice, and there stood—his mother!

Frank had often dreamed of seeing her beside him, but he knew it was no dream now when his mother's arms were round him, and his tired head could rest on her dear shoulder.

There was no fear of his being angry, but a pang of jealousy shot through Floride's heart as she watched them together. They were so wrapt up in each other that they did not even see her. She picked up her basket, and was about to steal away, when Frank lifted his head from its resting-place, and said: "Mamma, it's Floride, my little nurse."

Then Mrs. Laine smiled at her radiantly, and putting an arm around her, said: "My dear little girl," in a way that meant more than all the thanks in the world.

"Have you come to stay?" asked Frank, eagerly, and when she answered, "Yes, my darling," he sank back on his pillow, worn out with excitement, but perfectly happy.

109

It was some time before he opened his eyes again, and then he looked at Floride, and said, brightly: " I'm going to get well now."

And he kept his word.

A RELIC-HUNTER'S STRANGE EXPERIENCE

The Tale of a Mysterious Bombardment

RANK MORELEY had scarcely passed from his last skirts to his first trousers when he became known as the most persistent " collector," in his native town. He began, under the direction of his mother, with pressed flowers; then in succession he collected marbles and tops; a year later his assortment of birds' eggs were envied by every boy in town, and he afterwards exhibited at the county fair a collection of stuffed birds which attracted the attention of a prominent naturalist. Of course he attempted to collect coins, and was finally discouraged by the expense of securing a " full set " of anything—even American cents. When he grew old enough to write in manly fashion, he spent all his pocket money for stamps and stationery with which to solicit autographs of distinguished personages.

When the Civil War broke out Frank importuned every volunteer of his acquaintance to send him something—it mattered not what —from fort or field, and as he was himself an obliging fellow, his acquaintances responded so freely that Frank's room soon looked like a junk-shop, or a museum constructed from the contents of a rubbish heap.

Finally Frank grew old enough to go to the war himself, and from that time forward he addressed himself to his favorite pursuit with an industry that was equally amusing and amazing to the veterans among whom he was a recruit. Nothing came amiss: a bit of the saddle-cloth of a distinguished general; a broken bayonet from an abandoned Confederate camp; a green cotton umbrella which an escaping slave said had belonged to an ex-Governor of Virginia; two bricks which Frank himself extracted from the wall of the Colonial powder-house at Williamsburg; a shingle from a house in which Washington was said to have passed a night, were among the treasures which Frank brought into the tent, only six feet square, in which he and three other soldiers lived while in camp.

Frank's comrades merely laughed at these things, but when the young collector endeavored to make room for an entire window-sash, five feet wide, two feet high, and full of diamond-shaped panes of glass of the last century, the other inmates of the tent objected so strongly that Frank had to bribe a hospital steward to secrete the precious " find " under an invalid's bed.

What troubled the young soldier most, however, was that he was unable to secure any real war relics — mementos of great battles. His regiment, like most others in the cavalry service, did much hard work, but seldom —indeed, never, during Frank's early martial days—took part in a hard fight. But one day the Confederates made a reconnoissance in force towards the little post at which the —th Cavalry was stationed, and there was much powder burned, particularly by a Union gunboat, which steamed up a little river on one flank, and fired many shells over the woods at the enemy.

After the latter retired, and the cavalry returned from a rather late pursuit, the regiment halted near the scene of the late engagement, and Frank improved the opportunity to scour the field for relics. His search was abundantly rewarded, for he found several unexploded shells, most of them very large. To carry them all to camp was impossible, but Frank was fertile in resources, so, after rolling one 30-pounder shell in his overcoat and strapping it on his saddle-bow, he lugged the others to a bit of woods behind the abandoned house in which the picket reserve was always quartered, laid them in a row on the ground, placed rails from a neighboring fence on each side and on top of them, and then covered the whole with brush-wood, an immense heap of which was close by.

" There !" said the relic-hunter to himself, when his work was completed, " I don't believe any other collector will ever find them. Whenever I happen to be detailed for picket duty at this post I can take one back to camp with me, and some day I'll find a way to ship them all home. What a fine lot they'll make to exchange with other collectors for different things when the war is over !"

About a fortnight later Frank was roused from deep slumber in the middle of the night by the self-explaining bugle-call of "boots and saddles." The regiment mounted quickly, and went at a gallop through the little town, and out in the direction of the recent reconnoissance and fight. Nobody knew what was the matter, but on passing the cavalry picket station itself—guided, apparently, by the light of a fire which somebody had made in the woods. Why they had not fired more nobody knew, but there had been enough to justify an alarm of the entire post, and to establish the belief that fighting would begin in bloody earnest as soon as day dawned. So the cavalry remained "to horse" all night, and a blacker or more rainy and utterly miserable night Frank had never known. At daybreak the cavalry advanced, a section of artillery being with the advance, and scoured the country; but not a native — not even a friendly negro —had seen one of the enemy within a fortnight.

It was very strange—it was also very wearisome; so as soon as the regiment was again within the picket lines the colonel ordered a halt and rest. Frank was fearfully sleepy; he was also hungry; but he was consoled by the thought that now he could secure and carry to camp one of his hidden relics; so he made his way towards the woods behind the station.

He did not find the brush heap, nor even the rails, but just where he had hidden the shells— he was certain as to the place, for it was very near an old pine-tree with a peculiar axe-mark on the trunk—was a hole as large as a cellar, and beside it stood the colonel of the regiment and the captain of the picket guard. They were in earnest conversation, and Frank heard the colonel say:

"I never heard of such extraordinary artillery practice. You say the fire in the woods was just here?"

"The very place," said the captain. "There was a great brush heap here, and some fellow set it on fire, I suppose, while lighting his pipe. Of course when we saw it there was no way to extinguish it."

"I suppose not," said the colonel; "but how could the enemy have got the range so exactly? They must have used the same gun each time, and plumped their shells in exactly the same spot."

"That isn't possible," said the captain. "Some of the explosions were much louder than others, so there must have been guns of different calibre."

"It's a mystery," said the colonel, after eying the hole all over, as if looking for an explanation. "I can't understand it at all."

"I can," said Frank to himself, turning abruptly and walking away. "I see it all. That brush heap took fire, the fence rails burned, too, the shells became red-hot, and one by one they burst just where they lay. And that is the end of the finest collection of war relics I ever saw. Oh, dear!"

Then, like a dutiful soldier, Frank started back to tell the colonel how the supposed shelling of the station occurred, but he met the officer sauntering back to his command, and looking so tired and cross, as the result of a wakeful night, that the young soldier quickly concluded that he would wait for a more appropriate time. Rejoining his comrades, Frank thought that he would at least tell somebody, but a full half of the men were asleep, and the others were saying such dreadful things about the enemy who had been mean enough to keep two or three thousand men awake all night without the privilege of trying to get even in the morning, that the young relic-hunter again determined to say nothing until a better time occurred.

So he kept his secret for more than twenty years, and then he accidentally met his old colonel, took him home to dinner, showed a lot of relics he had picked up in the later years of the war, and then told him the story substantially as it is told here.

CLARE'S RIDE

How a Boy Saved the Third Troop

THE FOURTH CAVALRY is a fine regiment, and has won a splendid reputation for coolness and courage; but of all its achievements, it is prouder of none than Clare's ride. In the first place, it really was a gallant undertaking, and one that the boldest veteran might have shrunk from; then, Clare was only twelve years old at the time, which was in the old days of Indian fighting in the West. Clare's father was a captain of the Third Troop, which was stationed at Fort Beaver, a small frontier post in the White River country. Clare's mother was dead, and since his ninth year the boy had lived with his father at the fort.

Though, of course, not a regularly enlisted member of the regiment, Clare regarded himself as belonging to it. He wore the uniform, turned out to guard mount at daybreak, attended drills, and performed the duties assigned to him with the promptness and precision of an old soldier. Clare's father believed that the discipline of military life would be of service to the boy in after years. It must be admitted that when roused out of a sound sleep by the bugle-call on a cold winter morning, Clare would gladly have turned over in his warm bed for just one more nap. But he remembered what his friend, Sergeant Tom, once said: " If a man is afraid of the weather, what will he be when it comes to bullets ?" And so, though he yawned, rubbed his eyes, and shivered a good deal, he was never late at roll-call.

There was not a man in the regiment who did not love the little fellow, with his frank, serious face, and his quaint, dignified air. And not one of them but saluted him as respectfully as if he had really been an officer. It was because they knew that from the tips of his small cavalry boots, with their jingling spurs, to the crown of his blue cap, with its crossed sabres, Clare was a gentleman, and would sooner have lost his right hand than tell a lie or carry a tale. "If that boy," remarked Sergeant Tom, "should say that he had seen a drove of elephants out on the plain yonder, I should believe him, for it would be true."

During Clare's three years' experience as a soldier, the Indians had remained quiet, and the most exciting event which had occurred in all that time was a chase after strayed cattle, in which he had taken part. But now there began to be rumors of trouble. The Sioux on the neighboring reservation were said to be preparing for war. Clare noticed that his father looked grave, and that there were frequent consultations between the officers. The stockade, or high wall of logs driven into the ground and bolted firmly together, which constituted the defences of the fort, was repaired and strengthened. Rifles and sabres were cleaned and polished. Sentries were doubled on the platforms overlooking the plain, and strict orders were issued, forbidding any soldier to leave the fort.

From his bedroom window in the upper story of the officers' quarters, Clare often saw wild-looking figures, in plumed head-dresses, careering swiftly to and fro on their wiry little ponies, far off on the prairie. Miles away, below the level horizon-line, tall columns of smoke rose up against the blue sky, and melted into the clear air. Sergeant Tom said that these smokes were signals, by means of which the scattered parties of Indians communicated with each other at a distance.

Day after day went by, and Clare began to think that the Indians meant no harm, after all. He saw, too, that his father and the other officers looked more cheerful. Only Sergeant Tom shook his head, and said: " Wait !"

One afternoon Clare sat in his room working out an example on his slate. It was warm, and the whirring of the locusts in the long grass of the prairie coming through the open window made him drowsy. Two or three times he nodded over the table, and at last he must really have fallen asleep, for the next he knew there was a sudden tumult of shouts and cries, trampling of hoofs, and firing of guns. Then came the quick, sharp notes of the bugle sounding the alarm.

He ran to the window and looked out. The whole plain seemed alive with Indians, wheeling and galloping hither and thither. Some of the men on the platforms were firing over the edge of the stockade; others were hurrying across the parade - ground, buckling on their belts as they went. In the middle of the open space he saw his father, with his sword drawn, looking very calm and brave as he issued his orders.

With his heart beating rapidly, Clare put on his cap and ran down-stairs. At the door he met Sergeant Tom, who smiled as he saw the boy.

" Well, lad," he said, " you are going to see some real soldiering now. Are you frightened, Clare ?"

" A little," admitted Clare.

" That's because you are not used to the business," said Sergeant Tom. " When you have seen as many skirmishes as I have, you won't mind a bit of a brush like this." And shouldering his rifle, he marched off toward the stockade, as erect and cool as if on drill.

After their first repulse, the Indians drew back out of range of the marksmen in the fort, but apparently with no intention of giving up the attack. Spreading out in such a way as to surround the stockade on all sides, they dismounted from their ponies, placed sentinels to keep a close watch upon the movements of the whites, and prepared to camp for the night.

The sun went down, and darkness stole slowly over the wide surface of the prairie. Never had the sight seemed so solemn to Clare, and for a moment his stout little heart sank in his breast, and the tears welled into his eyes. But he dashed them away, with a feeling of shame; for there, on the platform beneath his window, was Sergeant Tom, pacing to and fro, with his rifle on his arm, whistling softly as he walked. Nevertheless, he could not shake off the gloomy thoughts that had seized him, and presently he resolved to go down and talk with his father.

When he reached the bottom of the stairs, however, he heard the sound of voices in his father's room. As he turned to go up-stairs again, he heard his own name mentioned. It was his father who was speaking.

" If it were not for my poor little Clare," he was saying, " I could face it better. I should have sent him away at the first rumor, but no one believed that there would be any serious trouble."

" You think that we are in a tight place, captain ?" said another voice.

" You can judge for yourself," responded the captain. " The Indians number fully five hundred, and we have but thirty men to defend the fort with."

" There are the six troops at Stanley, only twenty miles away."

"It might as well be two hundred, for we have no means of getting word to them in time. According to the custom of these Indians, we shall be attacked in force at daybreak to-morrow, and against a combined rush we could not hold out half an hour."

"With your permission, captain," said a voice which had not hitherto taken part in the conversation, "I will make a dash for it. With a good horse—"

"Impossible, lieutenant! You would not go a furlong. No; we must do our best to beat them off until help arrives."

There was a long pause. "Let us go to our posts, gentlemen. If the worst comes, we can but do our duty."

Clare crept up - stairs, and sat down in the dark to think. For a time he was sick with the terror of what he had overheard; then his courage began to come back to him, and with it a great resolve. *He would save the fort!*

A day or two before he had discovered by chance, at the foot of the stockade behind the stable, a hole which, by a little digging, he could enlarge sufficiently to crawl through. He had meant to speak of this hole to Sergeant Tom, but in the excitement of the attack he had for-

125

gotten to do so. He was glad of it now, for that hole was an important part of the plan he meant to carry out.

At some distance from the fort there was a deep ditch or gully, probably the bed of a dried-up creek. Looking from his window at sunset, Clare had observed at the bottom of this gully a number of horses, fastened by halters, belonging to the savages.

Now the whole surface of the prairie was covered with tall, thick grass, and a person passing through the hole in the stockade might, with great caution, work his way to the gully where the horses were. This was Clare's plan.

Pulling off his boots, with their noisy spurs, he crept softly down-stairs in his stocking-feet. Keeping in the shadow of the buildings, he managed to reach the stockade unseen by those within. It was the work of a very few minutes to dig away the soft earth so that he could squeeze through. Once outside, the real danger of his attempt came upon him with overwhelming force, turning him faint. But he resolutely shook off his weakness, and began crawling towards the gully on his hands and knees.

That terrible journey seemed long hours to Clare. Every instant he expected to hear the yell of discovery and the whiz of a rifle - ball. Once, indeed, he was very near detection. One of the Indian sentinels sauntered past within a dozen feet of where he lay prone in the grass. Hardly breathing until the sound of the man's footsteps died away, he resumed his crawl, and in a few minutes more found himself on the edge of the gully.

He slid softly down, and approached one of the horses, tied a little apart from the other animals. Fortunately for Clare, it was not an Indian pony, which might have been unruly, but a well-broken horse, stolen from some white settler. It had neither saddle nor bridle, but Clare was used to riding bare-back. Leading the animal slowly down the gully until he believed himself at a safe distance, he urged him up the sloping bank to the plain above, mounted him, and set off at a wild gallop. The events of that strange ride seemed like a dream to Clare, and he could hardly realize that he had done the twenty miles, when the sharp challenge of the sentry caused him to pull up his steaming horse.

" Clare! You here alone at this time of the night!"

It required but a dozen words to explain his

errand. The major in command of the detachment was a thorough soldier, and in a very few
minutes two hundred stout troopers were in
their saddles, and, led by the major, beside
whom rode Clare on a fresh horse, they started
off at a sharp trot.

Clare was tortured by the dread that the relief would arrive too late. Every now and then
he glanced anxiously at the eastern horizon for
signs of the coming dawn.

"Take it easy, Clare," said the major, in response to the boy's request that the speed of the
squadron should be quickened. "Those rascals
won't attack till daybreak, and we shall get
there in time to catch them in the rear and do
them up nicely, never you fear."

And so they rode on over the silent prairie
under the large stars, with thumps of hoofs,
creaking of saddle-leathers, and jingle of bits
and spurs. At last Clare's quick eye detected
a pale, milky glow low down in the eastern
sky; and now they were within a mile of the
fort. Making a détour to avoid the gully which
Clare had crossed, the detachment was halted
under cover of a slight rise of ground.

Brighter and brighter grew the glow in the
east, until the stern features of the men, drawn

128

up in two long lines, were visible in the gray light. Suddenly the far - off whiplike crack of a rifle came to their ears on the gentle morning air, followed by a continuous rattle. The attack had begun.

The major straightened himself in his saddle, and drew his sabre with a clang. " Quick, march !"

The men moved off steadily, increasing their pace as they rode. Rounding the hillock, Clare saw hundreds of dark figures rushing towards the stockade, from the top of which sprang a wavering fringe of fire. He heard the major give an order in a loud, stern voice; then he was whirled onward in a mad confusion of rearing horses, shouting men, crashing guns, and flashing sabres.

He remembered nothing more distinctly until he heard some one crying, " Shoulder high !" and found himself being borne through the gates of the fort by a dozen cheering men, among whom he recognized Sergeant Tom, with powder-blackened face, waving his cap and yelling like an Indian.

Later, when the enemy had been driven miles over the prairie, and scattered in every dircetion, the men were drawn up in lines on the parade-ground, and calling Clare to his side, the major made an address which caused the boy to turn very red, though it was not to be denied he felt very proud, too.

After this, Sergeant Tom, stepping out of the line, said: " Three cheers for Clare! Now, then, with a will!"

The roar that went up shook the very colors on the flag-staff, and rolled far and wide over the prairie. Then the bugle sounded a lively air, and the men dispersed to their quarters, and Clare, his father, and the major went to breakfast.

And this was Clare's famous ride.

HOW HO-TO-OTO BECAME A RECRUIT

The Tale of an Indian Soldier

T was a cold, dismal day in early summer. The wind blew sharply from the north, the sky was dark and cloudy, the ground wet from the morning's sleet. Old Chief Troyka, driving home from the mission church, buttoned his long coat more tightly about him, and with a disgusted " Ugh!" at such uncomfortable weather, plied his whip vigorously over the backs of his two rough-coated cayuses. The ponies, on feeling the lash, looked, if possible, a little more unhappy than an Indian pony usually looks, but otherwise scorned to notice the indignity, and steadfastly refrained from hastening the gait they had themselves chosen. So Troyka, feeling unequal to a contest with them just then, gave another grunt of discontent, and settled back in his seat beside his passive squaw.

Wenatchee was not only passive, but was, in spite of disagreeable weather and obstreperous ponies, perfectly content. And why should she not be? Was she not arrayed in a new green woollen dress, with a tasteful blue shawl over it, and a wonderful " store " hat with red feathers? And wasn't she holding aloft a tremendous green cotton umbrella—up for neither sun, rain, nor snow? But, then, every one doesn't possess umbrellas, and though Wenatchee was not unduly proud, she did love to display her fine possessions. And above all else, was she not seated in the springy wagon by the side of her lordly husband, instead of trudging along the road, as she had done in days gone by? Indeed, Wenatchee had nothing to complain of. Moreover, she had not Troyka's main cause of discontent. She knew well that neither weather nor ponies were disturbing the old chief, nor were his thoughts dwelling upon the sermon or the church they had just left. She knew that they were hovering angrily and painfully about the unpainted log cabin next to the church — the gloomy " skookum - house," in which at that moment his sister's son Ho-to-oto was confined.

It was only last week that old Holos-nin, a neighbor of Troyka's, who bore the chief a lasting grudge because he had once caused his son to be sent to the skookum-house for petty theft, met Troyka on the road by the agency, and said:

"How! Troyka! A cattle-thief is worse than a plough-thief, isn't he?"

"Much worse," replied Troyka, astonished.

"And gets a longer time in the skookum-house, doesn't he?"

"Much longer. But you know, Holos-nin. Why do you ask?"

"I only wanted to remind you of it, so that you wouldn't forget when you came to try your sister's son Ho-to-oto for stealing my cattle— three of them."

"Stealing your cattle? Ho-to-oto? What do you mean, Holos-nin?"

"What I say. They've been stolen, and sold to a butcher in Davenport."

"Well, Ho-to-oto didn't do it."

"Who else did, then; tell me? Who would do it but Ho-to-oto, that good-for-nothing, lazy Indian, who spends his time wandering over the plains while we are ploughing our land? We'll see what the other judges think!"

" They can think, and you can talk, Holosnin; but it will take more than your word to put Ho-to-oto in the skookum-house. It will take a witness."

So Troyka had answered in his indignation, but his heart had been troubled, and when Wenatchee had chimed in afterwards, with abuse of Ho-to-oto for bringing disgrace on his mother's brother, he had said nothing.

For Ho-to-oto *was* idle. He wouldn't go to school, and he wouldn't work. Ploughing and reading were alike distasteful to him. The wild flowers grew on his barren, unbroken land, and his ragged tepee fluttered in the wind in sight of his neighbors' well - built houses. And because of these things the rest of the tribe had a contempt for him. For they were a civilized, thrifty, self - respecting group of Indians, who tilled their own farms, raised their own crops, sent their children to the mission school, and drove to church every Sunday in their own spring wagons and buckboards.

And Troyka was the big man of the tribe: the largest cattle-owner, the most prosperous farmer, and one of the three judges, as well as hereditary chief.

And now this proud old man, who had always respected himself and held his head so high, was to suffer disgrace through his nephew; for Holos-nin had found a witness, and the Indian police had accordingly brought Ho-to-oto into the agency the day before, and confined him in the skookum-house to await his trial the following Saturday.

Ho-to-oto had not stolen the cattle, for he was honest, if he was idle, and at first he had laughed at the accusation; but when he heard there was a witness against him, he grew troubled, for he had spent the whole day wandering, gun in hand, over the brown, barren plains that he loved, and he had not seen an Indian who could testify where he had been.

He wished now, for the first time in his life, that he had stayed at home instead and ploughed his land, where the scrubby " grease-wood " of the prairie still grew. If he had only heeded his uncle's advice, and sometimes worked a little, instead of always following his own desires and going hunting or fishing!

Fishing! Ho-to-oto strained his ears to hear the roar and rush of the river below as it swept along, swirling past the rocks, dashing up against the big cliffs, and tossing about the great logs on their way down to the Columbia as though they were mere bits of bark. When could he stand on the rocks in mid-river again?

It didn't comfort him much in his imprisonment to know that his uncle, who was fond of him and believed him innocent, would be one of the judges. If the other two found him guilty, the majority would rule, and he would have to be punished.

And Ho-to-oto knew what the punishment would be — a long imprisonment in the skookum-house, shut away from the sunshine and the wide sweep of the prairies; away from the foaming water and the gleaming fish; where he could not feel the fresh air on his cheek or hear the wind making strange sounds through the pines, or roam at will over the hills.

Those were bitter thoughts to Ho-to-oto, yet even they were forgotten in the one bitterest thought of all—they would cut off his hair: his long, straight, black hair, that hung in thick, matted strands half-way to his waist, would be shorn, and the short, stubby ends would tell of his disgrace long after he would be out of prison.

The day of Ho-to-oto's trial dawned bright and fair. Early in the morning all the Indians of the tribe came thronging into the agency. A strange, picturesque-looking crowd they were, the men with their long hair, and the squaws in their many-colored clothes. Indeed, these latter were wonderful to look upon, in skirts of every hue, with bright red, green, or purple plaid shawls and brilliant handkerchiefs, topped with gay head-cloths or still gayer hats.

But the Indians were not the only ones who were to be present at the trial. Over in the fort across the river a young cavalry officer swung himself on his horse and cantered swiftly down the line, followed by a stiff, solemn-faced sergeant, also on horseback. He was bound for the agency, under orders from his commander to see if he could induce any of the Indians to enlist as soldiers.

As the two men clattered down the long, steep hill to the river, the Indians, having tied their horses to the fence around the agency, passed into the court-room. The three judges took their seats on the platform at one end of the room, old Troyka in the middle, and an Indian policeman was sent to the skookum-house for the prisoner.

137

Ho-to-oto came and stood at the left of the judges, sunk in despair. Then, all being present, old Holos-nin was ordered to tell his story. Just as he commenced, the riders from the post reached the bridge, and after stopping a moment to breathe their horses, began the ascent on the other side.

When Holos-nin finished his long - winded account, Ho-to-oto was asked what he had to say. In a hopeless tone the poor fellow told how he had gone off that day far beyond Huckleberry Mountain and the big swamp, and had not gotten back until ten at night. Now Huckleberry Mountain was in exactly the opposite direction from the little town where the cattle had been taken to be sold, and no one could possibly get to both places on the same day. So one of the judges asked:

"Did any one see you going to Huckleberry Mountain, Ho-to-oto? Have you a witness to prove you were there?"

"A white man, a soldier, saw me," replied Ho-to-oto, drearily. "He was hunting, too, and I sold him four birds. I don't know who he was."

Several Indians in the room grunted contemptuously at this, and Holos-nin laughed.

"Have you a witness, Holos-nin?" next asked the judge.

"Yes," replied the old Indian. "Here he is," whereupon a young Indian in a brown coat stepped forward and told how he had passed Ho-to-oto driving the three cattle into·Davenport.

The judges looked grave; Troyka's heart was troubled, and Holos-nin laughed again. He thought Troyka wouldn't hold his head quite so high after his sister's son was imprisoned.

At that moment there was a clatter in the doorway; a young cavalry officer and a solemn-faced sergeant came clanking into the room, accompanied by the Indian agent.

Ho-to-oto started forward, laughing himself now. "There he is!" he exclaimed, pointing to the new - comers. "There's my witness! There's the soldier who bought my birds!"

"Hullo!" exclaimed the sergeant, who didn't understand a word Ho-to-oto was saying. "Excuse me, sir, but that's a young chap who sold me some birds a week or so ago. He seems to be talking to me. What's it about, John?"

At this the Indian agent spoke up, and after

translating what the agent had said, asked the judges of what Ho-to-oto was accused.

Explanations followed amid much excitement, and before long the brown-coated Indian, who afterwards turned out to have been the thief himself, was detained as prisoner in Ho-to-oto's place, and Ho-to-oto was set free.

He didn't exult loudly; he simply walked out of the court-room, and seated himself on a log outside to think.

It had come home to him forcibly what a poor opinion the tribe had of him, that no one had volunteered a word in his behalf, and his heart was very sore.

Lost in his thoughts, he didn't notice that any one had approached till he felt a tap on his shoulder, and looking up saw the friendly face of the young officer and the solemn sergeant, and heard the agent ask him if he wouldn't like to be a soldier.

And so it came to pass that one bright, sunny day, two weeks later, old Troyka and Wenatchee got into the spring wagon again, and drove down to the bridge and up the steep hill to the post. And there, out on the green parade-ground, in all the glory of his uniform, was Ho-to-oto, marching and counter-marching, and bending and kneeling, and pointing his gun this way and that, in company with some half-dozen other Indian recruits, under the command of the young officer.

Troyka was immensely proud now of his sister's son as he gazed at him in his trim blue suit and important air. And as for Wenatchee, her opinion of him completely changed at sight of the brass buttons, and she chanted his praises in her soft, guttural tones, as enthusiastically as she had formerly abused him.

Ho-to-oto himself had learned a lesson, and showed it by his determination that the army should not suffer through any laziness of his. His drill was a serious matter with him; his uniform was even more serious; and as for his short hair—well, it is one thing to have your hair cut off because you are considered a thief, and quite another to be shorn for glory's sake, to mark you a soldier—a noble Indian recruit of the United States army.

"SCAPEGRACE"

A Story of a Great Railroad Strike

THERE was one boy at Fort Ransom who was foolish enough to wish that there were no such things as women in the world, and that was Captain Grace's ten-year-old Tommy. There weren't very many of them in Tommy's own world, to be sure, and yet there seemed to be so many from without "coming in and interfering with a feller," as he expressed it. We all know the old adage, "What is everybody's business is nobody's business," but Tommy—on the principle probably that it was a poor rule that wouldn't work both ways—had long since made up his mind that people read the thing t'other side foremost, and, so far as he was concerned, what was really nobody's business seemed everybody's business.

It was nobody's business, for instance, that

he should like to wear a little beaded buckskin shirt that his father had made for him among the Sioux Indians, but the mothers of other boys in the garrison, boys who hadn't a Sioux hunting-shirt, used to come to Captain Grace, or to Aunt 'Ria, and protest against his being allowed to run wild in such heathenish garments.

It was nobody's business, thought Tommy, that he should prefer to spend his holidays four miles away from the fort, among the railway men at the round - house, where all the locomotives of the division were in turn "stabled" and oiled and cleaned and fired; but other boys were not allowed to go, and, boy-like, upbraided their mothers, who accordingly upbraided Aunt 'Ria. It was nobody's business that his father gave Tommy for his own purposes the stupendous sum of twenty-five cents a week for spending-money, stipulating only one thing—that not a cent should ever go for cigarettes; but there were many good and devout women at the fort who declared to Aunt 'Ria that this was simply throwing money away, and snaring the youngster's path with temptation. "No boy of mine," said more than one mamma, "shall

143

ever be allowed to carry about him the means of indulging vicious tastes." And no one was more decided on this point than the chaplain's good wife, whose own boy had been the means of making Tommy acquainted with cigarettes the year before.

In fact, it was because of his refusal to contribute more than one-fifth of his weekly allowance to the fund for the Sunday-school Christmas Tree that had led the lady superintendent to refer to him as *Scape* Grace, instead of Tommy. "Give a dog a bad name," said the adage, and as with a dog so with a boy. Fort Ransom took up the name with a zest which was born of a propensity for teasing rather than any spirit of unkindness, but it stuck, as often will the most undeserved of names or reputations, and Tommy Grace, through no real fault of his own, became the scapegrace of the big garrison.

It was anything but fair to the little fellow. He was just as square and honest and well-meaning a boy as there was in the whole community. Ransom was quite a large post, far out across the wide, wind-swept prairies of the West, and near the bustling railway town of Butteville—generally named Butte for short. Here were stationed during the year gone by the headquarters and eight companies of a regiment of " regular " infantry, and one of these companies was commanded by Captain Grace. Tommy's lot might have been a very different one but for a fact you have probably already surmised—that he had lost his mother. Five years before, when he was a little bit of a chap, a severe and sudden illness had swept her from their sight almost before they could realize that she was in danger. Tommy was too young to know what he had lost, but the blow was a bitter one to his soldier father. Not for long months did he return to the regiment after taking her to her far-away Eastern home for burial, and when he did the captain brought with him his sister, a maiden lady of nearly his own age, the only thing in the world he could think of as a partial substitute for Tommy's mother.

Aunt 'Ria had no experience in taking care of children, but she had all manner of theories as to how they should be reared and managed. 'As a result poor Tommy's early boyhood proved to be a period of curiously varying experiments. What was right and proper for him to do one month was all wrong the next, and by the time he was ten years old his ideas of boy rights and wrongs might have become hopelessly confused but for his own propensity for taking the bit in his teeth, and bolting for advice and comfort to his father himself.

"Never mind what the trouble is, Tommy —never mind whether the fault is yours or somebody else's—never be afraid to come and tell me the whole story just as 'straight' as you know how. Let me be your best friend, and I'll do my best; only remember, Tom, 'the truth, the whole truth, and nothing but the truth.' I don't care what mischief you can get into or wrong you can do so long as you tell me all about it. Concealment is what I should fear most."

"Poor little chap!" he said to himself, "he has no mother to go to and sob out his troubles. Boys hate to cry before their fathers, especially soldier boys. I can't be his playmate, for boys must have boys for that, but I can be his friend, please God! and teach him to trust me and confide in me, and if he does get into scrapes they can't be any worse than mine were."

And so, despite his name, Tommy wasn't particularly miserable except when Aunt 'Ria was lecturing, or "those other women" were telling him about what he should be or shouldn't be doing, " if you were my boy." Captain Grace had taught him to stand respectfully and listen to it all in silence, " just as I do, Tommy, when the colonel finds fault with something in Company B, or when I'm officer of the day."

" But *he* has a right to," blurted Tommy; " he's commanding officer. Now Mrs. Croly and Mrs. Wilson and Mrs. Darling, *they* haven't any business telling Aunt 'Ria or me I shouldn't do this or that so long as you approve."

" Never mind, Tommy. Every woman thinks she has," said the philosophic captain. " It does them good. It does you no harm, and we have lots of fun over it between ourselves. So never be rude or disrespectful."

The division superintendent at Butte was a man just the age of Captain Grace, and from early boyhood the two had been close friends. Even after their separation, when young Grace was sent to West Point, they had kept up their correspondence, and great was the captain's pleasure when the regiment was ordered down " out of the Sioux country " and stationed at Ransom, mainly because it brought him once

147

more into close relations with George Rollins, his old - time school chum and his life - long friend.

Promotion in railroading is almost as slow as it is in the army, and Mr. Rollins at forty was only a division superintendent, but every one connected with " the road " was well aware that better things were in store for him. Rollins was still a bachelor, and he took instantly to Master Tommy, and for a whole year that little man had been learning all the mysteries of the round - house, the shops, the train-despatcher's office, and " the road " generally, for while on Saturdays, and even, it must be owned, on occasional Sunday afternoons, the captain and his old friend were chatting together over old times, Master Tommy, perched in the cab of the switch-engine under care of " Mike " Farrell, the engineer, was steaming up and down the yards, darting from track to track, shunting cars from shop to station, from storehouse to elevator, making up trains and pulling them hither and yon, and all the time his eyes and ears were wide open, and he was practically bent on " learning the business."

Farrell taught him the purpose and use of every lever, rod, stop-cock, and gauge about the engine; let him ring the bell, whistle for brakes or switches; even, after a while, let him stand on the engineer's instead of the fireman's bench at the side of the cab, and with Farrell's brawny, hairy fist to guide, seize the throttle-valve with his own boy hand and start the engine, increase the steam, and shut it off. He learned how to make a " gentle " start without jerk or strain; he learned how to reverse and " back," although he had not strength enough to throw the great geared lever that Farrell handled so easily. He learned all the science of " firing," so far as it could be taught on a switch engine, and later Mr. Rollins handed him over to the engineer of the great transcontinental express trains, and bid Ned Weston, who ran No. 615, the biggest and most powerful passenger locomotive on the mountain division, take him on his Saturdays as far west as Summit Siding, away up at the top of the range, and there present him to " Hank " Lee, whose engine, No. 525, made the daily down-grade run with the East-bound mail—a light, swift train— from Summit to Butte in forty-seven minutes. That was a glorious run, and Tommy loved to tell of it; so much so, that other boys, and lots of them, grew tired or envious, or both; and

11   149

even while secretly wishing that they knew the division superintendent, and that he would give them " the run of the road " as he did Tommy Grace, they feigned to scorn the whole business, and to ridicule Tommy's railway friends, and sneer at his aims and aspirations—for Tommy had long since decided he did not mean to be a soldier; he was going to be a locomotive engineer.

" If I were Scapegrace," said one of his best friends among the boys, " I'd shake books entirely and stick to the round-house; he's learned that lesson, anyhow."

" If I were Captain Grace," said the schoolmaster, " I should require Thomas to spend his Saturdays studying what he has missed during the week, instead of wasting time among those railway hands."

" And if I had any influence with Captain Grace — or if Miss Grace had, either — something would be done to redeem that poor little fellow," said more than one of the army mothers at Ransom. " Think of the danger he is running."

But Captain Grace was deaf to protests of this nature. He listened to what was said with his quiet smile, spent his hour with Tommy every evening over the slate and books, satisfied himself that what the boy did know he knew thoroughly and well, and almost every Saturday rode into Butte with him, and was there to meet him when No. 4 (the mail train) came clanging into the station late in the afternoon, Tommy's cinder-streaked, chubby, happy face smiling at him from the cab.

" That boy's going to be a boss engineer one of these days, captain," said Mr. Lee one lovely May evening. " I shouldn't wonder if Mr. Rollins would have to start him as a fireman before he's fourteen. The road 'll be glad to get a boy as bright as Tommy. He can handle this old lady now most as well as my fireman here," and Hank patted affectionately the massive steel connecting-rod of his " driving-wheels."

But neither engineer, nor captain, nor Tommy dreamed how soon, how very soon, " the road " and all Fort Ransom would devoutly thank Heaven that Scapegrace had learned railroading better than he had arithmetic.

Leaving only a small detachment to guard the fort, Colonel Wallace, with the regiment, early in June, had marched away westward from Ransom, had crossed the mountain range, and had joined a force of infantry and cavalry massed in the valley of the Beaver, ninety miles away. There they were to spend two months in manœuvres under command of a general officer, and there, right after the Fourth of July, some of the boys were to join their fathers in camp—Tommy among them.

But late in June came tidings of serious troubles among the railway men at the East; then the news that a general strike was threatened, and all of a sudden some mysterious order was flashed along the wires even to Butte and beyond, and that day not another wheel turned on the mountain division. In vain Mr. Rollins argued and pleaded with his men. They honored him—they had no " grievance " with their employers—but one and all they were members of some one of the several railway men's " Unions," sworn to obey the orders of their respective chiefs, even against those of their foremen or superintendents, and the firemen, switchmen, and certain trainmen had received the signal to strike, and though in almost every case it was done with misgiving and reluctance, strike they did.

Then the engineers tried to run their engines with new hands for firemen, even in some cases tried to " fire " for themselves. Then committees came and warned the new-comers off, and such as would not obey were promptly pulled off and kicked out of the yards. The next who tried were stoned and beaten. Then deputy marshals were called to protect the newly employed, and then came riot. It was bad enough at Butte, where the station and yards were in the hands of railway men alone, but it was infinitely worse in great cities to the east, where all the criminal classes, the mass of tramps, loafers, and vagabonds promptly turned out. The next thing known at Ransom a million dollars' worth of railway property was being burned and destroyed; the police and the sheriffs were beaten, and the President ordered the " regulars " to the scene.

Never will the boys of Fort Ransom forget the evening of the 2d of July, when the despatch was received that Colonel Wallace, with his eight companies, on a special train, had started from Beaver Station, and would pass through Butte, eastward bound, at ten o'clock that very night if *nothing interfered.* There was a military telegraph line running from Ransom through Bear's Paw Gap, miles north of the railway, and so on through the mountains to the outlying forts in the Beaver Valley.

That, as yet, at least, the strikers had not cut; but, all too soon, they learned, through friends and sympathizers among the railway telegraphers, that Mr. Rollins had been able to make up a train; and with old No. 615 in the lead, big Ned Weston at the throttle-valve, two of Uncle Sam's bluecoats for firemen, and Captain Grace with six of his men to back Mr. Rollins on the engine and tender, and with the whole train bristling with bayonets, Colonel Wallace and his regiment were coming for all they were worth, bound to carry out their orders if they had to cut their way through Butte.

It was the nervous schoolmaster himself who rushed out to the fort, and drove the women and children wild with fear and excitement over the next news—that the strikers had armed themselves, and that, with the hangers-on and the unemployed about the town and the great array from the repair-shops, a thousand determined men had gathered, and meant to assault the troop train—" if, indeed," said he, " it ever gets as far as Butte. If a possible thing, wire to Summit siding and warn them." And wire the quartermaster did, only to get reply: " Too late. Troop train passed through at nine o'clock. Should be at Butte now."

"Oh, if we only had Scapegrace with us now!" was the wail of one poor wife and mother. "Is there *no* way of warning? He knew every bit of the track to the west. He should have ridden out and done something." All the other boys were safe at home within the fort gates, but not since evening gun-fire had Tommy been seen. "He took his pony, ma'am, and galloped away to Butte like mad just before sundown," was all the quartermaster sergeant could tell Aunt 'Ria, before he himself mounted and rode away after the quartermaster in the vain hope that it might not yet be too late to " do something."

Down in the bottom of his heart the quartermaster had no dread of any serious trouble once the troop train got to Butte. Old Wallace knew very well how to handle mobs, big or little; but that long stretch of lonely, unprotected track through the foot-hills to the west, that wooden trestle, that Howe truss-bridge over Four-mile Creek, suppose the strikers were to get there first, and wreck them in front of that heavy train thundering down grade. *There* was the rub!

And Scapegrace had not had his eyes and ears open for six long months for nothing. No sooner had he heard the talk at Ransom of how a special train was to come on and break the blockade than he bethought him of stories he had heard in cab and caboose, in switchman's shanty and carsmith's shop, and never did that piebald pony split the wind as he did on Tommy's dash for town. Leaving him panting and astonished at the corral, his little master, wellnigh breathless himself, made his rapid way to the depot. The platforms were crowded with rough, sullen, angry men. Somebody was making a speech, and urging the crowd to stand together now, and sweep the bloody-handed soldiers from the face of the earth if ever they strove to pass the spot; and then some frantic, half-drunken fellow shrieked: " They'll never see this side of Four-mile Run!" And Tommy, wild with anxiety, sought in vain for some familiar, friendly face, for some one to tell what *had* been done or advise what he should do. All in vain. Engineers had been driven from the yards and forbidden to return. The striking firemen, appalled most of them by the proportions assumed by the riot, seemed to have slunk away. These wild, riotous, half-drunken men were total strangers. Perhaps it was lucky that they knew him no better than he knew them, or he might not have slipped, trembling, away, as he was enabled to a moment later, his boy heart fluttering up into his throat, for the fearful words he heard had stricken him with terror.

"I tell you 'twarn't no use to burn the bridge ahead of 'em. They'd only ford the creek, march into town, and make up a train here, an' we hadn't the men to stop 'em. There was only just one thing to do — to set them switch signals 'All right, come ahead,' and wreck the whole outfit as it reached the bridge."

Ten minutes later, his young heart bounding like his pony's hoofs, Scapegrace was galloping westward over the broad prairie, leaving Butte a mile behind, and Ransom farther still beyond. Already darkness was settling over the foot-hills of the range; already lights were popping up here and there from outlying ranch or farm-house. Behind him the electric globes were gleaming high over the bustling town, but Tommy had no time to look back. Half a mile to the southward he could see dim lights, like will-o'-the-wisps, dancing along what he knew to be the railway embankment, and ahead of him, dark, gloomy, vague, and silent, lay the broad valley through which turned and twisted

157

the stream. A roaring mountain torrent at times, it was only " bank full " now. There was a low wooden bridge two hundred yards north of the railway trestle; there was a good ford a quarter of a mile above that, but if by any chance these were guarded by the strikers —and Tom had heard how they held them long years before in the great railway strike of '77 —then he and Dot would either have to push a full mile farther up stream or find some un-guarded point and swim for it. In his right hand he carried a lantern, borrowed at the cor-ral—taken, rather, without a by-your-leave to anybody—for only a Mexican packer was there as he unhitched his pony. In his pocket were his matches, and on his lips a prayer for aid and guidance and protection.

Beyond all doubt those twinkling lights far to the left and front meant that the strikers were already at the trestle and the truss. Be-yond all doubt the only thing for him to do was to pass around them to the north, and speed far and fast up the winding ravines among the foot-hills until—a sure, safe distance beyond all chance of interference—he could light his lantern when the great blazing eye of No. 615 came peering forth from the black mouth of the tunnel, and then he would leap on the track and signal the engineer to stop.

Not three miles from town, and already Dot was panting and protesting. Not yet quarter past nine, but black darkness was settling down over distant peak and neighboring prairie.

One mile farther and he would reach the bridge, but long before coming to the stream he must pull up and go cautiously and listen. How dreadfully near those dim, wicked lights looked at the southwest — away down in the lowlands! Something told him what they meant. All that ground was overflowed in the spring. The truss-bridge and the trestle carried the track along full twenty feet above the July level of the stream, and, just as they said at the depot, these villains out here were sawing slanting cuts through the sturdy beams—the uprights of the trestle—and the weight of the massive engine would do the rest. *On*, Dot! — on! Even now old 615 must be roaring through the rock cuts east of Summit. Tommy could even seem to see his friend the engineer standing there with firm - set face staring straight ahead through the cab window, his right hand on the reversing-lever, his left on the air-brake cock, the throttle-valve shut

159

tight, and not an ounce of steam on, for with smoking wheels the great train was shooting curve after curve down the east face of the grand mountain spur, held back from headlong rush to destruction only by the grip of the brakes on the polished steel of the tires. And soon they would plunge into the tunnel through Ute Tower, and then come sweeping forth in long, graceful curve around Red Bluffs, and then, then Ned's left would shift from air-brake to throttle, and one would close and the other open, and 615 would begin again to throb and puff and pant, and, with unhampered wheels, the long train would leap to the race once more, with Four-mile Creek and switch and siding, and beyond them the big truss and trestle only two level miles ahead.

Heavens! Here was Four-mile Creek now, foaming along almost parallel with his road, and there, not two hundred yards ahead, lay the low uncovered wooden bridge over which he must pass unseen, or else ford or swim. Many a time, with exultant heart, high aloft, had he gone skimming over that dimly outlined trestle and under that net-work of beams and stringers just visible against the southern stars. Many a time had he and Dot ridden over the humble crossing that seemed to span only from rock to rock—a fragile bridge that was swept away every spring, only to be gathered up and put together by the ranchmen every June, but on the trestle twinkled wreckers' lights. On the low bridge ahead gleamed a lantern that told him the enemy was there. Dot almost slid upon his haunches in astonishment at the sudden check, and then whirled madly about in answer to his rider's driving heel and tugging rein. Springing up from the roadside a few yards ahead, a dark form loomed suddenly into sight, and a hoarse voice shouted: " Who's *that?*"

But Scapegrace never stopped to answer. With his head turned homeward Dot took new heart, and flew back along the lonely road full three hundred yards before he felt the pressure of leg and rein that turned him northward. Indignantly he shook his mane, but obediently sped away. Over the springy bunch-grass he was laboring now, panting hard, and wondering what on earth could make his little master so unmerciful, and presently there were sounds as of distant shouting, at which Tommy urged the more, and bent low over the pommel, and then Dot found himself circling westward again, but far above the point where first they reached the bank of the stream, and soon he heard it roaring over its rocky bed and straight ahead of them. Another moment and he would have swerved, for here they were upon the very verge, but both Tommy's heels came driving hard against his astonished ribs, and Tommy's knees were gripping him like a living vise. One instant he faltered at the brink and then plunged helplessly in, yielding to the master hand and will. " *On,* Dot!—on!" was Tommy's constant cry. And so, stumbling, plunging, going down once on his knees, and burying his nose deep in, the gallant piebald obeyed, and at last, with dripping flanks, clambered safely out on the westward side. One short minute for a breathing spell, then on they went again. Four minutes more, and the dim lights at the bridge, half a mile to the south, were square to the left; six minutes, and they were well behind; ten minutes, and Tom and Dot, wearily, heavily now, were lumbering up a long ravine, dark and drear and lonely, but the brave heart of the little fellow never faltered; he would reach that level mile over the " bench " in front of Red Bluff, and stop the headlong rush of old 615, no matter what lying switch lights might say, no matter what drink-maddened strikers might do.

Already he was drawing near the track again. Glancing over his left shoulder he could see that only one light was gleaming now near the bridge—the faint green disk at the switch. Their cowardly work complete, the gang had doused their lanterns, and now were lurking in the shadows well away, yet lingering, fascinated, to watch the result. *On, Dot!—on!* It must be that the train is near. Scapegrace strained his ears to listen, but Dot's panting drowned all other sounds. At last, just ahead now, dimly seen against the southern sky, a straight lance-like staff stood pointing to the zenith — a telegraph pole, and there, farther east, another. The track at last—at last! and not an instant too soon. Even as he prodded Dot to one last effort, far to the west; among the hills, a dull roar as of distant thunder fell upon his ears. The train! the train! already at the Tower Tunnel.

In mad haste now he threw himself from the saddle, leaving Dot with bowed head and heaving flanks to look after himself. In mad haste he scrambled up the low embankment, grasping his precious lantern. In mad haste

163

he fumbled for his matches, thanking God with all his boyish heart that the night wind had not risen. Another minute, and, crack! a bright flame shot from the iron rail—another, and a feeble glimmer sprang from the wick. Another, and with increasing roar and rumble the bowels of the earth seemed to open slowly half a mile to the west, and a white light, growing every instant brighter and broader, came streaming around the base of Red Bluff, and then a brilliant gleaming eye seemed suddenly to focus on the track. Two threads of glistening steel, nearly five feet apart where he stood, seemed to meet almost immediately under it; the rails began to creep and quiver, the ground to tremble, and with his little heart away up in his throat Tommy lifted high his lantern—high as he could reach—then lowered and raised— lowered and raised, straight up and down— square in the middle of the track, and, bearing down on him at full speed, his mighty engine throbbing under him instinct with life, big Ned Weston, peering from his cab window just as Tommy pictured him, saw and understood. Shriek went the whistle, slap went the throttle- valve flat against the boiler, snap went the air- brake, every clamp gripping its wheel on the

"A BREATHLESS BOY STUMBLED FORWARD INTO THEIR ARMS, SOBBING OUT: 'THE BRIDGE!'"

instant like a vise. Out from the 'scape-valve, with mighty hiss and roar, rushed the pent-up steam, and all of a sudden the big train began to bump and grind along the rails. Black heads popped out of the open windows, and little by little old 615's flying wheels slowed down and came to a stand, and Ned Weston's foremost guards springing from the pilot, ran ahead, a tall captain bounding after them, and a little freckle-faced, breathless boy stumbled forward into their arms, sobbing out: " The bridge."

Four hours later, in another train, without a man injured or missing, Colonel Wallace and his command pushed ahead from Butte. Meantime, however, they had marched into town with half a dozen prisoners, picked up near the ruined trestle, had hammered some riotous heads rather hard, and had had a chance to tell to many a wife and mother who had hurried into town for one glimpse of her own particular soldier the story of their escape. " Goodness gracious!" said Fort Ransom, " who would have thought of that in Scapegrace?"
But it was the old colonel who picked the little fellow up and held him close to his heart one minute before they started on again, then,

with glistening eyes, returned him to his silent father, and grasped the latter's hand. "Say, rather, who would have thought of that but Scapegrace!" was the way old Wallace put it.

THE SURRENDER OF COCHISE

A Gallant Messenger of Peace

WAS about to tell General S. S. Sumner a story about a brave boy who became war chief of the Crow Indians, when he told me a more interesting tale. We were talking about courage and gallant men, and General Sumner said that a very brave Indian once told him that General O. O. Howard was the bravest man he ever saw.

The circumstances were these. Down in Arizona and in New Mexico, in 1872, the terrible Apache Indians had been committing frequent and bloody crimes, robbing and murdering white settlers, and fighting our soldiers. One band of these unruly redskins was, at the time of this story, hidden away in the Dragoon Mountains, under the command of a fierce and stalwart chief named Cochise. General Howard was in that corner of our country on an errand of peace! He was visiting the various savage tribes, and trying to reason with their chiefs, in order that they could be brought to see that it would be better for them to stop fighting and go on reservations. That seems a strange errand for a soldier, and especially for such a valiant fighter as General Howard, who, before that, had lost an arm for his country, and won fame on more than one battle-field.

Strange as it was, that was what General Howard was doing—going from tribe to tribe in plain citizen's clothes, and trying to reason with the wildest Indians on the continent. A motley crowd followed him, and he brought together husbands and wives and children, who had been separated in the fighting and retreating and chasing of the Indians by the troops. He was kind and gentle, and was beloved by those who came in his way. And he had a great deal of success in quieting some tribes and putting them on reservations where they might live peacefully.

It was said to be impossible to find the great chief Cochise, who was hidden away in the mountains. To tell the truth, nobody else had any desire to see him, for he was notorious as a fierce foe of the white people, a turbulent leader of a murderous band of " Apache devils," as his Indians were well called. It was not only hard to see Cochise, but it was as much as any white man's life was worth to be seen by him. He had been massacring the settlers, and was hiding from the punishment he deserved, and getting ready to make more mischief. But General Howard wished particularly to meet him, and when he heard that a man named Jefferds knew the way to Cochise's hiding-place, the general employed the man to take him there.

Jefferds was a man who served as a guide and as a scout for our soldiers, and knew that country well. He agreed to take the general, and off they went across mountains and plains and other mountains, and finally to a third range called the Dragoon Mountains. When they neared the desperate Indian's hiding - place, Jefferds said that the general had too many people in his train; for a lot of Indians were trooping along with the white men to join their tribes, and some were squaws and children belonging to Cochise's band. Jefferds said that if Cochise saw so many people he would fight them. The general asked how many it would do

169

to go with, and yet not alarm the suspicious chief. Finally, it was agreed that the general, his companion, Captain Joseph A. Sladen, Jefferds, and two Indians, making five in all, should form the party. The others were then left behind, and the five rode on—to death, as some of them thought.

Captain Sladen asked the general if he did not realize his danger. He asked whether the general was not aware that he was almost certain to be killed. General Howard replied by quoting the Bible. He recited a verse which says that if we lose a life for our Saviour's sake, we shall have an eternal life given to us. Captain Sladen rode on in silence. It seemed wonderful that General Howard should ride straight into that Indian trap, where Indians were hidden behind the rocks, and where a white man's life was not worth a fig. And yet he wore no uniform, and carried no weapon except a tiny penknife.

Straight into Cochise's stronghold went the general and his men. It was a fort made by nature: a place of forty acres in extent, walled all around by great rocks, and with only one opening in the wall for any one to get in or out. There were hundreds of Apaches in there—at

"'I WANT PEACE MYSELF,' SAID COCHISE"

least three hundred, if I remember rightly. They all surrounded the white men, who were made to understand that they were prisoners. Worse yet, they were told that Cochise was going to make up his mind during the day whether to kill them or no. Cochise did not show himself. The general and his companions had all that day and all that night in which to think of what they had done, and what were their chances of ever seeing their homes again. Escape was utterly impossible. At night they spread blankets on the ground under some trees and slept. How many of those who read this would have slept that night under those circumstances? But these men got a good night's rest.

On the next day Cochise made his appearance. He heard through an interpreter who General Howard was, and that he came to make peace.

" I want peace myself," said Cochise. The tall, muscular Indian spoke only Spanish and Apache. He was a very large, fine-looking man, and seemed a giant among the Apaches.

" If you want peace," said General Howard, " we can soon arrange it." He talked no nonsense about " the Great White Father at Wash-

ington." He simply said: " There are two parties of white men. One is now in power.
That party wants peace with the Indians. The
President of the United States sent me to see
you."

When it was agreed that Cochise and his
warriors and squaws should go down from the
mountains and live upon a reservation which
the general agreed to give them, near Apache
Pass, the wily chief shook his head.

" When I go with you the soldiers will shoot
my people," he said.

" But I will order them not to," said General
Howard. " I will send Captain Sladen."

" They will not care what he says," said the
chief, " but they will obey you. You go and
order them to leave us alone. Leave Captain
Sladen here. My women will take good care
of him."

So the general went and left the captain in
that terrible trap. Then it was that the general
saw General Sumner, then lieutenant-colonel,
and arranged for a meeting between Cochise
and the officers in command of the troops that
were stationed out there. Even then Colonel
Sumner doubted the intentions of Cochise. The
Apaches are a treacherous lot, and have not

taught the white men to trust them. Colonel Sumner would not have been surprised if the redmen had massacred all the officers when they had a chance. But the colonel admits that General Howard seemed unconscious of any danger. He was honestly trying to bring about peace, and he seemed to think of nothing but peace. In this case his faith was justified, for Cochise went upon a reservation, and remained " a good Indian " until he died, but many another man who has trusted other Apaches has died for doing so.

Cochise had a wise head on his shoulders. " I notice," he said, " the more white men I kill, the faster they come, and the more there are of them. It is no use to fight them. I will do as they tell me."

Long afterwards he told Colonel Sumner how surprised he was to see General Howard ride into his stronghold. " Me think I am a brave man," he said, " but General Howard the bravest man me ever saw."

On the other hand, if the reader should ever ask the general about his adventures, he would smile and say:

" Oh, I knew Cochise was not going to kill me when I hunted him out. The little children came and lay on my blanket, and played around me when I was a prisoner there. They would not have been allowed to do so if I was to have been killed."

WITH CAPRON AT EL CANEY

A Day of Real Battle

ON the night of June 31, 1898, I lay down to sleep with the very comfortable feeling that my hopes, cherished through many tedious days of hardship, were at last to be realized. For my blanket was spread, along with the blanket of another long - suffering correspondent, on a knob of a hill overlooking El Caney, a small village in southeastern Cuba, and we all knew that El Caney was to be stormed by our troops in the morning. The prospect of seeing a battle was enough to make up for all the difficulties and privations, necessary or unnecessary, which we had endured, and we were not discomforted even by the thought of stray bullets, which often find correspondents as satisfactory billets as they do soldiers. We dreamed of our names in heroic head-lines in the daily papers, of deeds of might and valor, of captured standards, of flying Spanish soldiers — and we were quite happy. We changed our opinion, later, by the way, about those "flying Spanish soldiers."*

The hill upon which we were bivouacked was to be occupied by Captain Capron's battery of field-artillery, according to the plans for the action of the morrow. It is about a mile and a half to the south of the village. The guns had not yet been put in position, but they were

---

* Brigadier-General Vara del Rey, the Spanish general in command at El Caney, offered the most stubborn resistance which the Americans encountered in the whole Santiago campaign. His force of only a little over 500 men held their ground almost all day, and the Americans killed and wounded numbered 438. General Lawton's total force in the afternoon was 226 officers and 4913 men. The Spaniards had been told by their officers that the Americans would give no quarter. In spite of some aid from the gallant Captain Capron's small field-battery, this engagement was practically an attack by infantry upon a strongly fortified, well-armed enemy, which is always costly. Of the Spanish force it is estimated that not over forty escaped. The others were killed, wounded, or taken prisoners. General del Rey was shot while rallying his men in the streets of the village of El Caney, a short distance behind the fort. No more gallant officer fought on the Spanish side, and if he had been in supreme command at Santiago our victory would have been more difficult. A superb eighteenth-century bronze cannon has been mounted on a high pedestal within the battered walls of the stone fort at El Caney as a memorial of the action and a monument to the dead.— EDITOR.

concealed in some woods, just beyond the brow of the hill. We could hear the horses every now and then crackling the twigs of the underbrush as they lay down to rest. Indeed, this was almost the only sound which broke the stillness of the night. In cautious silence Captain Capron, his lieutenants, my companion, and I ate our cold hardtack and bacon — fires had been forbidden—and turned in for sleep, after sentinels had been carefully posted to guard against surprise by Spanish scouting parties. Every precaution was observed to prevent the enemy from obtaining a knowledge of our whereabouts.

For protection from the heavy tropical dew we had spread our blankets under the boughs of a gigantic mango-tree. Sleeping under a mango-tree is like sleeping on a bed of tennis-balls. But we were too worn out to make much of an effort to clear the ground of the fruit which thickly covered it, and having done our best to adjust our bodies to the situation, we were just dozing off to sleep when the land - crabs arrived on the scene. With these pleasant creatures we were forced to fight a pitched battle in order to drive them away, and as my eyes were finally closing for the night I heard what was evidently a brisk skirmish with the land-

crabs going on where the privates were dreaming—or trying to.

It may have been hard to get to sleep that
night, but it was an easy matter to wake up
the next morning. At the very first glimmer-
ing of dawn the camp is all astir. The privates
roll and stow away the blankets and equipment,
and the guns are slowly wheeled into position.
Ammunition - boxes are made ready and un-
screwed. Officers set to work with delicate
range - finders, determining and recording the
ranges of various landmarks along the lines to
be attacked. A squad of men goes out in front,
cutting away the shrubs and small trees which
might obstruct or confuse our fire. As the sun
gets up, the older hands in command begin to
roll up sleeves and "lighten ship." To our
rear we can see the columns of the First Regular Infantry taking up their position to act as
our support in case of need. Clearly, this battery is intended to do business.

As the light grows, we look curiously at the
country to the north. The little town, with its
small, white block-house, looks almost patheti-
cally helpless when we consider that it is surrounded by nearly 5000 men. Occasionally one
can catch glimpses of soldiers among the houses

and about the block-house, but, for the most part, there are no signs of life there whatever. To the right and left our troops are stringing out through the woods. The various regiments take their positions without confusion or delay. General Lawton knows what he is going to do, and how he is going to do it. And he is too old and too good a fighter to go into action without a thorough knowledge of his fighting-ground. About the only reconnoitring done at all in the Santiago campaign was done around El Caney —and done by General Lawton himself.

As a vantage-point of observation, the hill on which we stood could not have been better chosen, affording a clear view of the valley in front and of the sweep of rising ground on either side. " The play is going to begin," said another correspondent to me, " and we've got front-row seats in the gallery." Besides being in the gallery, we were posted next to the man who was about to ring the bell to raise the curtain; for it had been ordered that the first gun from Captain Capron's battery was to be the signal for the battle to begin.

The men around the cannon are standing at attention; every piece has been shotted, and we all are in a quiver of expectation. Then the command rings out: "Number three, make ready! Fire!" The gun boomed in response, our first shell whistled its way towards the block-house, and a roll of smoke from our antiquated black powder drifted through the trees. Captain Capron has called "Time!" and the game has commenced.

. Now our infantry begins firing all along the line. The musketry fire sounds like a half-dozen gigantic corn-poppers. There is no advance apparent from our gallery—no inspiring charges, such as we had read about. The Spaniards, from behind the stone walls of El Caney, are keeping up a rattling, spitting fire. All of Capron's guns are now in operation, and the sulphurous, thick smoke hangs about us so that we can scarcely see. Some one says that a shell has exploded inside the block-house, and we cheer at this, and hope for a breeze to blow away the smoke so that we can make out what has been done. About ten o'clock the wounded begin to come back from the firing-line—limp, sagging, swaying figures, struggling to the surgeons. "It's hot down there," shouts one man, whom two others are carrying; "all-fired hot, and there ain't no Spanish runnin' yet, either." By this time we had pretty well filled the

" CAPRON'S BATTERY IN ACTION "

block-house with holes, and Captain Capron gave orders to train the guns on the houses in the village. Each one of these houses was a miniature fort, and it would have been impossible, without great loss, to have taken El Caney by assault until most of these houses had been battered down by our shells. So the gunners changed their aim, and the red tiles began to fly from the roofs.

It was nearly noon. The Spanish fire was as brisk and determined as ever, and, with the exception of the crumbling block-house, nothing had been apparently done to weaken it. We found out afterwards that we should have taken El Caney in one hour, according to headquarters' calculations.

But now through the tall, thick, hot grass in the valley we can see lines of men crawling slowly towards the village. Our firing-line is closing in; but it is an advance so different from the charges and rushes we have had pictured for us in war histories that we in the gallery hardly realize what is going on. Most of the time our men seem merely to be wriggling on the ground. Sometimes a squad stands up, makes a dash at a little rise of ground where there is thicker cover, and we have just time

13   181

to feel the thrill of a charge, when they drop again out of sight in the brush. But all the time they are going forward, and all the time the remorseless crackle of rifles is kept up without intermission.

It was easy to tell the whereabouts of the Second Massachusetts, both on account of the peculiar thick report which their old-fashioned rifles made, and because of the white smoke that rose after every volley. An old private in the Twenty-fourth (colored) Infantry said of the Massachusetts militia: " Yes, sah, they're sure 'nough nervy, but I ruther have a lot o' snowballs than them old muskets. It's murder to send them boys out those—jes murder."

And now the creeping blue lines have such a close grip on the yellow town that orders come to Capron to " cease firing," lest a " tumbler " drop in a company of our own men. One regiment, we can see, is within two hundred yards of the block-house. The soldiers are wading through the grass as if in deep water against a current, with bent bodies and out-stretched arms. El Caney and the Spanish pits about it flash and snap with rifle fire. How slowly our men go! They seem almost to be standing still; and yet the distance is growing less. Another regiment comes to their support. The crawling, crouching van is stopped by a fence—one of the barbed-wire devices of the Spaniards. Here they seem to halt for hours—really it is only a few seconds—and then we hear a faint, a very faint, cheering, and they break into a run up the steep slope and swarm up over the block-house, and we have planted our flag in the snarl-ing, fiery little village!

In the mean time Capron's battery had been ordered to a new position, but before well es-tablished there the town was ours, and my first battle was over. We had seen all that there was to see, and had experienced, to some extent, all the trials of warfare. During the last move-ment of the battery we had been under fire, and had been through a corner of the infantry battle-field where the dead and wounded were lying in pitiful plenty. And yet our real troubles were only beginning. A courier had come from El Pozo, and had told of the bloody confusion at San Juan, and of the urgent need of re-enforcements and of artillery.

Tired and worn out as we were, having fought all day and slept but little the night be-fore, we set out in the afternoon upon the San-tiago road. The First Infantry, in columns of fours, was at the head, and behind them came Capron's battery. The long line made an impressive sight against the background of deep green foliage. I remember particularly the picture of the men silhouetted against the sky when they were crossing an old stone bridge which spanned a sluggish stream in the valley. But I doubt if the picture made such an impression on me at the time as did the water of the brook, muddy and warm though it was. It was the first water we had drunk all day, and the weary, thirsty men tumbled over one another in their eagerness to fill their canteens.

At eight o'clock a halt was made, and the men lit fires along the roadside to cook the first meal they had made since morning. But it was not much of a supper. We were all more or less uneasy, as nobody seemed to know where we were going or where the enemy was. Every now and then the most alarming rumors would be passed down the road—that General Lawton had been shot, that the Spaniards had beaten our men at San Juan, or that our bivouac along the roadside was covered by a battery of Spanish machine - guns on the slopes above. The men with the battery tried to sleep, wrapping themselves in blankets, but although we did our best and were nearly worn out with fatigue, it was quite impossible.

It was three o'clock in the morning that an aide came galloping by with orders for the command to go back on the road over which we had plodded so laboriously the day before, and which now turned out, it was said, to lead squarely into the face of a Spanish battery. So, in the damp darkness, we wearily retraced our steps. It was very dismal business. The road was slippery with mud. Men and horses were completely fagged. Many had not slept for forty-eight hours. We had been through what to most of us was our first battle; all were hungry and exhausted.

Our countermarch was thus made. At daybreak rations were distributed, and the men were given a much-needed rest while breakfast was cooking. Then new orders were issued, and once more we fell in and marched towards the west, upon the right road at last for El Pozo, San Juan, and—Santiago.

ON AN ARIZONA TRAIL

A Prisoner and a Rescue

NEAR midnight of a late October day, many years ago, a lieutenant of infantry was sitting by a camp-table in his quarters at Fort Whipple, Arizona, reading a magazine. The walls of the room were formed of vertical pine logs, and the floor and ceiling of pine planks, all, logs and planks, lending a piny flavor to the room's atmosphere.

The mail from the Pacific coast, due once in two weeks, had failed to arrive a few days before, and a searching party sent to look for it had found the mutilated body of the cavalry expressman lying beside the trail in a deep gulch, and the mail matter torn and scattered over a broad space.

186

The dead soldier was brought in for burial, and the fragments of letters and papers gathered and taken to the quartermaster's office. Officers and men spent many hours in identifying and matching the soiled and ragged pieces. The lieutenant had worked diligently from noon till evening in making two magazines and half a dozen letters legible.

The fragments of each leaf were pasted on nearly transparent paper, the printed matter becoming fairly visible through its fibres. They were sorry - looking pages, however, at best. Many bits were gone, compelling the reader to supply by imagination scenes and incidents lost in the sage-brush and grease-wood bordering the La Paz trail.

The young officer occupied a leather-backed cross-legged camp-chair, which rose high above his reclining head, with his legs stretched across the bottom of a stool towards a generous fire of pine knots, which filled the room with a flood of light and drove out the autumnal chill. In this comfortable attitude, engrossed in a popular serial, he had passed away the first half of the night. He was just beginning a new chapter when he became aware of the distant and rapid clatter of a horse's feet. The sound came distinctly through the loop-holes in the outer wall of the room—loop-holes made for rifles and left open for ventilation. Dropping his book upon the table, he rose and listened intently to the hoof-beats. Some one was riding from the direction of Prescott, evidently in great haste; and as this was a country of alarms, the officer surmised that the rider was coming to the fort. The cadence of the gallop showed that the animal was a pony, and that he was being hard pressed.

A brief halt at the post of sentinel Number One and the galloping was resumed, the sound growing plainer, and showing that the rider had turned up the hill and was nearing the great gates now closed for the night. Presently the clatter of hoofs ceased, and the rapid breathing of a horse could be distinctly heard. The rider's feet came solidly to the earth, and an instant afterwards impatient fingers could be heard groping along the bark-covered logs in search of the secret postern—a gate made by sawing off a log close to the ground and attaching hinges to its inner side—usually left ajar except in time of danger. Then the impatient and discouraged voice of a boy exclaimed:

" Oh, why can't I find the gate !"

"OH! MR. RANDOLPH, THE INDIANS! THE INDIANS!"

" Seventh log to the right of the big gates! Push hard!" called the officer.

The immediate creak of hinges and rapid footsteps showed the rider had entered the fort and was approaching the room. The door swung suddenly open, and a handsome boy of about thirteen years entered, hatless, clothing soiled and torn, with bleeding face and hands.

" Oh, Mr. Randolph, the Indians! the Indians! They have attacked our ranch, and Aunt Martha is dead!" he exclaimed, as he sank exhausted on the stool.

" Attacked the ranch! When ?"

" About four o'clock."

" How many ?"

" Don't know. Seemed as if there was a hundred."

" But, Willie, you are wounded. Let me—"

" Never mind me—it's only a scratch. Send the soldiers, or Brenda and all the rest will be killed!"

" How did you get away from the ranch? But wait; I'll go for Captain Bayard and the surgeon, and then you can tell us all about it and save time."

Mr. Randolph had not far to go within the narrow limits of the stockade. The officers sought were asleep; but to his vigorous and excited summons they promptly arose, and in a few minutes were in his room, the surgeon bearing a small case of instruments.

Upon examination Willie's "scratch" was found to consist of a fracture of the radius of the left arm, made by a bullet, and a flesh-wound in the cheek, made by an arrow. Neither was a dangerous injury if properly treated. While Doctor Colton dressed the wounds the boy told his story.

Before he had gone far Captain Bayard asked Lieutenant Randolph to call the post adjutant, and upon the appearance of that official gave orders for a sergeant, two corporals, and twenty-two men to be got in readiness for immediate mounted service with rations for five days.

The fort was garrisoned by infantry only, a command containing many good riders, however, who were frequently mounted in an emergency requiring speed and short service. For this purpose a number of horses were kept by the quartermaster.

The command of the detachment was given to Lieutenant Randolph, and he at once sent a man to Prescott in advance, to secure the services of Paul Weaver and George Cooler, two accomplished scouts and hunters. They were asked to be in readiness to join the column when it should pass through the plaza.

Half an hour after the arrival of the wounded boy the men were in the saddle and on the way to Cholla Valley by way of the mountain trail. As they passed through Prescott — at that time a mere hamlet of rude log cabins— they found the veteran Weaver and the youthful Cooler, mounted on sturdy broncos, awaiting their arrival.

II

THE family to whose rescue the detachment was going had travelled one year before from Fort Wingate, New Mexico, to Prescott, Arizona, under escort of the soldiers now forming the Fort Whipple garrison. When Captain Bayard's command reached Wingate from the Rio Grande he found them awaiting its arrival, that they might make the journey under military protection. The name of the family was Arnold, and it consisted of a father and mother and three daughters, and a nephew and niece. The daughters were aged, respectively, twenty, eighteen, and sixteen, and the nephew and niece thirteen and fifteen.

Mr. Arnold waited upon Lieutenant Randolph, the acting quartermaster of the command, the evening before the march was resumed, and handed him a note from Captain Bayard, directing him to afford the bearer and his family all possible assistance on the march, and to see that their wagons were assigned a place in the train and their property guarded. The quartermaster's train consisted of eighty wagons and five hundred mules. There was also a commissary herd of three hundred oxen and a flock of eight hundred sheep.

At the first halt after leaving Fort Wingate Lieutenant Randolph called upon the Arnolds, and found the father, mother, and daughters gathered about a fire busy in the preparation of supper. Mr. Arnold was making a temporary table of the tailboard of a wagon and two water-kegs. He was a tall, well-proportioned man of dark complexion and regular features, with black, unkempt hair and restless eyes. He was clothed in faded and stained butternut flannel, consisting of a loose frock and wide trousers, the legs of the trousers tucked into the tops of road-worn boots. His hat was a broad-brimmed drab felt, battered and frayed. Mrs. Arnold sat on a stool, superintending the work of the family, her elbows upon her knees, holding a long-stemmed cob-pipe to her lips with her left hand, removing it at the end of each inspiration to emit the smoke, which curled slowly above her thin upper lip and thin aquiline nose, and replacing it for the next whiff. She was a tall, angular, high-shouldered, and flat-chested woman, dark from exposure to wind, sun, and rain, her hair brown in the neck, but many shades lighter on the top of her head. Her eyes were of an expressionless gray. A brown calico of scant pattern clung in lank folds to her thin and bony figure.

The three daughters were younger and less-faded types of their mother. Each was clad in a narrow-skirted calico dress, and each was stockingless and shoeless. Mother and daughters were dull, slow of speech, and ignorant.

The lieutenant stopped long enough to give some directions as to the observance of camp rules, the order of marching, how to prepare for waterless and woodless camping-places, what to do in case of attack, etc., and was about to turn away, when a clear, boyish voice called from the rear of a cedar-bush.

"Oh, lieutenant, may I speak to you a moment?"

Turning his horse in the direction of the voice the officer saw a boy approaching, switching a handsome riding-whip in his hand, a boy that made a good impression at once. In fact, the quality, modulation, and evident refinement of the voice had prepared Randolph before he turned for seeing just the bright, handsome lad that had now come up.

He was apparently about thirteen years old, neatly attired in a blue blouse and gray trousers, with russet-leather leggings and a waist-belt of the same material, from which hung a neat revolver and small pouch. A light felt hat sat on a well-shaped head, around which clustered closely cropped brown hair that showed a decided inclination to curl. Two honest blue eyes set in a bright and intelligent face looked smilingly up to the officer as he advanced.

"Yes," replied the lieutenant; "what do you wish?"

"Well, I don't know that you can help us, sir, but my sister's pony has lost a shoe, and we don't know whether we had better pull off the other three or let her wear them."

" Replace the lost one."

" That's not so easy, sir, with no spare shoes, and no blacksmith this side of Wingate."

" Have you never travelled with a government train before ?"

" No, sir."

" How do you suppose we shoe these five hundred mules that are drawing our wagons and constantly dropping shoes ?"

" Then you really have a blacksmith! But that will do us no good. Brenda and I do not belong to the government."

" But a part of the government belongs to you," replied Randolph. " Where is the pony ?"

" Over there behind the cedars. Brenda is giving her some sugar and corn - bread," answered the lad, pointing with his whip in the direction indicated.

" Get the pony and come with me, and we will see if ' Uncle Sam ' cannot spare a shoe for a niece's saddle-horse."

Returning thanks, the boy ran back joyfully, and soon returned leading a beautiful brown pony and accompanied by a young girl. The boy said: " Brenda, this is the quartermaster who is going to have Gypsy shod."

The girl bowed, and as the lieutenant sprang

from his saddle, instinctively doing homage to American girlhood, she extended her hand, saying: "I suppose we must consider that brother has introduced us."

"Yes, if 'Quartermaster' was my name," replied the lieutenant; "but I think you will find it more convenient during our long march to know my name." And he handed the girl a leaf from his memorandum-pad upon which he had written it. "One does not carry a card-case on a frontier march, you know. May I know your name?"

"It is Arnold," replied the girl.

"Not children of Mr. Arnold?—he told me he had three daughters only," and Randolph glanced from the neatly and well-dressed boy and girl before him to the three ill-clad, bare-footed girls at the camp-fire.

"No; we are a nephew and niece," Brenda answered. "If you will lend me your pencil and paper, I will exchange frontier-cards with you."

The pad was returned to the lieutenant with the names Brenda Arnold and William Duncan Arnold upon it.

The contrast between the two sets of cousins was something more than one of dress. The young girl before the officer was decidedly attractive in person, as well as refined in speech and manner. How she could be even remotely related to the Arnold daughters at the camp-fire was difficult to comprehend. She was a blonde, with abundant tresses of flaxen hair held in a leash of blue ribbon, and a delicate complexion which the journey had tanned and sprinkled with abundant freckles, giving promise of rare beauty with added years and less exposure to sun and wind. The boy was a self-reliant little fellow, who exhibited a refined brotherly courtesy towards his sister, a reflection of good home training.

The Arnold history, incidentally gathered by Randolph during a month's march, was briefly this: Brenda and William were the children of Mr. Arnold's only brother, and had been reared in a large inland city of New York. Their father and mother had recently perished in a railway accident, and the children had been sent to the paternal uncle in Colorado, who was believed, as he had always represented himself, to be in affluent circumstances. There were relatives on the mother's side, but they were scattered, two of her brothers being in Europe at the time of the accident. Brenda and Willie had reached their Western uncle just as he was starting on one of his periodical moves—this time to Arizona.

The different social status of the families of the two brothers was unusual but not impossible in our country. One of the brothers was ambitious, of steady habits, and possessed of a receptive mind; the other was idle, impatient of restraint, with a disinclination to protracted effort of any kind. One had worked his way through college, had entered a profession, and married well. The other had drifted through States and Territories — a rolling stone that gathered no moss—and had married the daughter of a nomadic Missourian.

The pony Gypsy was shod by the soldier blacksmith, and the boy William who led her to the travelling forge was informed that the train contained representatives of many useful trades, and that he and his relative were welcome to any services the command could render.

On the daily marches it was the custom of Lieutenant Randolph to ride in the rear or beside the wagons. The infantry marched out briskly every morning, never getting far in advance; but it was rarely seen again by the rearguard till the next camping-place was reached.

198

The wagons of the Arnold family travelled between the guard and the government wagons. They consisted of two large canvas - covered " prairie - schooners," drawn by three pairs of oxen each, beside which four cows, four horses, and four dogs were usually grouped. The father and the eldest daughter drove the ox-teams; the mother, the two remaining daughters, and Brenda rode the ponies. William walked, or rode in a wagon, except when one of the cousins, his aunt, or Brenda chose the wagon and let him have a horse.

As soon as Lieutenant Randolph noticed that the boy was dependent upon the charity of others for a ride, he made him happy by giving him an order on the chief wagonmaster for a spare mule with saddle, bridle, and spurs. Accordingly he appeared one morning mounted on a little buff-colored mule with zebra stripes on shoulders, hips, and knees, and accompanied the lieutenant during the day's march. The following day Brenda joined her brother, and for the rest of the journey the two usually rode with Lieutenant Randolph.

The route abounded with game, and in sections where the column was secure from Indian attack the lieutenant taught the boy and girl the use of rifle and pistol with fair success. The instruction began in camp, where they were taught the mechanism of their arms and target practice.

Brenda soon overcame her natural timidity for firearms, and became a successful rival of her brother when shooting at inanimate objects; but pity for birds and beasts prevented her from being a successful sportswoman.

The niece always acted as applicant whenever the Arnold family desired a favor from their military escort. One day, when the train had pulled out of camp, the two young attendants did not join their friend as usual. He did not give the circumstance serious thought, supposing their absence was caused by some domestic accident or delay; and not doubting but he would presently hear the clatter of the pony's and mule's hoofs as Brenda and her brother hastened to overtake him, the lieutenant continued to ride on.

He had gone nearly a mile when a corporal of the guard ran after him, and reported that the Arnolds had not hitched up, and were still in camp. Halting the train and guard, Randolph went back and found Brenda sitting by the roadside in tears.

"What is the matter, Miss Arnold?" he asked.

"Oh, it is something this time," she sobbed, "that I think even you cannot remedy."

"Then you think I can generally remedy things? Thank you."

"You have always helped us so far; but I do not see how you can now."

"What is the trouble, please?"

"Our poor oxen have worn their hoofs through to the quick. They have been obliged to travel much faster and longer distances, in order to keep up with the military train, than they ever did before. And the gravel has worn out their hoofs. We must remain behind."

"Perhaps things are not so bad as you think. Let us go and see," said the lieutenant.

"But we must go slower, Mr. Randolph, or the feet will not heal. Uncle says so. And if we drop behind the soldiers, who will protect us from the Indians?"

Rising dejectedly, and by no means inspired by hope, Brenda led the way to the Arnold camping-place, where the officer found the father and mother on their knees beside an ox, engaged in binding rawhide "boots" to the animal's feet. These boots were squares cut from a fresh hide procured from the last ox slaughtered by the soldiers. The foot of the ox being set in the centre, the square was gathered about the ankle and fastened with a thong of buckskin.

"Are all your cattle in this condition, Mr. Arnold?" asked Randolph.

"Only one other's 's bad 's this; but all of 'em's bad."

"That, certainly, is a very bad-looking foot. I don't see how you kept up with cattle in that condition."

"Had to, or git left."

"That's where you make a mistake. We could not leave you behind in any case. You must go with us, somehow, for you would not last a day in this region if we left you behind."

"I didn't think 'twould be of any use to say anythin'," said Mr. Arnold. "You seem t' have all you can haul now."

"We have three hundred head of oxen in our commissary herd that used to belong to a freighter. We can exchange with you. A beef is a beef."

"Thank you, lieutenant. I didn't think you could do it."

" That's easy enough. Turn your cattle into our herd and catch up a new lot. When we get to Prescott you can have your old teams if you want them."

" Thank you, again. I shall want them. They know my ways and I know theirs."

" Here, Willie!" the officer called to the boy. " Bring up your zebra and take a note for me to Captain Bayard."

A note was written and despatched to the commanding officer, detailing the circumstances causing the halt, and the action taken by the writer to enable the immigrants to go on. Half an hour later the prairie-schooners were again on the road, and joy reigned in the Arnold hearts. Frequent changes of draught animals were afterwards made, until the close of the march, when Mr. Arnold's stock was gathered from the drove and returned to him in fine condition.

When the soldiers arrived at Fort Whipple, or rather the site of that work—for they built it after their arrival—the Arnolds made their home for a short time in Prescott, and then removed to a section of land which they took up in Cholla Valley, ten miles to the west by the mountain trail, and twenty - five by the only practicable wagon-road. This place was selected for a residence because its distance from Prescott and its situation at the junction of the bridle-path and wagon-road made it an excellent site for a wayside inn.

Parties from the fort frequently passed the Arnold ranch during the stages of selection, building, and cultivation, and the officers took much interest in inspecting the arrangements for comfort, and the devices for making a defence against possible Indian attack. The house and stables were built of pine logs, squared and laid up horizontally, the windows fitted with thick shutters, and the doorways made to resist forcible entrance. Loop-holes for firearms were made in the walls and temporarily filled with mud.

In case the house became untenable an ingenious earthwork was constructed twenty yards from it, which could be entered by means of a subterranean passage from the cellar. This miniature fort was in the form of a circular pit sunk four feet into the ground and covered by a nearly flat roof, the edges or eaves of which were but a foot and a half above the surface of the earth. In the space between the surface and the eaves were loop-holes. The roof was of heavy pine timber, closely joined, sloping upwards slightly from circumference to centre, and covered by two feet of tamped earth. To obtain water a second covered way led from the earthwork to a spring fifty yards distant, its outer entrance being concealed in a rock nook shrouded in a thick clump of willows.

This history of the Arnolds explains the tragedy which brought Willie to the fort. While his arm was being set and wounds dressed, and preparations being made for the expedition, he told the officers all that had happened at Cholla Valley on the day of the attack up to the time of his departure.

A party of forty-one Apaches had appeared in the vicinity of the ranch near the close of the afternoon, and had spent an hour or more in reconnoitring the valley and its approaches. Apparently satisfied that they would not be interrupted in their attack by outside parties, they began operations by collecting the cattle and horses, and placing them in charge of two of their number near the spring.

Next they fired one of the out-buildings, and under cover of the smoke gained entrance to a second which stood less than one hundred feet from the north side of the house. Knocking the mud and chips from between the logs here and there, they were enabled to open fire upon the settlers at short range.

With the first appearance of the Indians, Mr. Arnold, assisted by two travellers who had arrived that afternoon from Date Creek on their way to Prescott, closed the windows and doorways with heavy puncheon shutters, removed the stops from the loop-holes, directed the girls to carry provisions and property into the earthwork, got the arms and ammunition ready, and patiently awaited further demonstrations.

The available defensive force consisted of every member of the family and the two strangers. The mother and daughters had been taught the use of firearms by the husband and father, and Willie and Brenda by Lieutenant Randolph. In an emergency like the one being narrated, where death and mutilation were sure to follow capture, the girls were nerved to do all that could be expected of boys of their ages.

Until the Apaches gained possession of the second out-building few shots had been exchanged, and the besieged closely watched their movements from the loop-holes. It was while doing this that a bullet pierced the brain of Mrs. Arnold, and she fell dead in the midst of her family. Had the two travellers not been present, the demoralization which followed the death of the mother might have enabled the savages to reach the doors and gain an entrance; but while the family was plunged in its first grief, the strangers stood at the loop-holes and held the assailants in check.

The body of Mrs. Arnold was borne to the cellar by the sorrowing husband, accompanied by the weeping children. The firing became desultory and without apparent effect. Bullet and arrow could not pierce the thick walls of the log house. Only through the loop - holes could a missile enter, and by rare good-fortune none of the defenders, after the first casualty, chanced to be in line when one did.

The family again assembled in defence of their home and lives, the grave necessity of keeping off the impending danger banishing thoughts of their bereavement, in a measure. An ominous silence on the part of the Indians was broken at last by the swish of a blazing arrow to the roof. Mr. Arnold rushed to the garret, and with the butt of his rifle broke a hole in the covering and flung the little torch to the ground.

But another and another followed, and in spite of desperate and vigilant action the pine shingles burst into flames in several places. At this juncture, Willie, whose station was on the south side of the house, and who had for some time been looking through a loop-hole in that direction, approached Mr. Arnold and said:

" Uncle Amos, I see Gypsy grazing near the spring, close by the willows, and the two Indians there keep well this way, watching the fight. If you will allow me, I will creep through the passage, mount, and ride to the fort for the soldiers."

Mr. Arnold took a long look through the aperture and replied: "God bless you, William; I think there's a good chance of your doin' it. If Brenda's willin', you may try it."

Brenda's reply to the proposition was to throw her arms about her brother's neck, kiss him, and without a word go back to her station. The lad silently took leave of his uncle and cousins, and dropped into the cellar. Passing into the earthwork he took a bridle and saddle, buckled on a pair of spurs, and crept through the passage to the spring. Standing in the screen of willows he parted the bushes cautiously on the side towards the Indians, and saw them, over a hundred yards distant, standing with their backs towards him, watching the house, the roof of which was now a roaring, leaping mass of flame.

Closing the boughs again, Willie opened them in an opposite direction, and crept softly up to Gypsy, holding out his hand to her. The docile pony raised her head, and, coming forward, placed her nose in his palm, submitting to be bridled and saddled without objection or noise.

Leaping into the saddle, the boy drove his spurs into the bronco's flanks, and was off at a furious gallop in the direction of Whipple. Startled by the hoof-beats the Apaches looked back and began running diagonally across the field to try to intercept the boy before he turned into the direct trail. Arrow after arrow and one bullet sped after him, one of the former grazing his cheek, and the latter fracturing his arm.

It was dusk when Willie began his ride, and it grew rapidly dark as he hurried along the bridle-path. Neither he nor the pony had been over this route before. Twice they got off the trail, and long and miserable hours were spent in regaining it; but the fort was reached at last, and the alarm given.

III

With twenty-eight men, including the two scouts and post surgeon, Lieutenant Randolph left Prescott for Cholla Valley. The night was moonless, but the myriad stars shone brilliantly through the rare atmosphere of that Western region, lighting the trail and making it easy to follow. It was a narrow pathway, with but few places where two horsemen could ride abreast, so conversation was almost impossible, and few words, except those of command, were spoken; nor were the men in a mood to talk. All were more or less excited and impatient, and wherever the road would permit urged their horses into a run.

The trail climbed and descended rugged steeps, crossed smooth intervals, skirted the edges of precipices, wound along the borders of dry creeks, and threaded forests and clumps of sage-brush and grease-wood. Throughout the ride the imaginations of officers and men were depicting the scenes they feared were being enacted in the valley, or which might take place if they failed to arrive in time to prevent.

It is needless to say, perhaps, that the one person about whom the thoughts of the men composing the rescuing party centred was the gentle, bright, and pretty Brenda. She had been a conspicuous figure and a daily companion on a march of over four weeks' duration, and they had frequently met her since their arrival and location at the post. Her uniform courtesy and fine appreciation of the slightest service rendered her had won the esteem and respect of every soldier in the command. To think of her falling into the hands of the merciless Apaches was almost maddening.

On and on rode the column, the men giving their panting steeds no more rest than the nature of the road and the success of the expedition required. At last they reached the spur of the range behind which lay Cholla Valley. They skirted it, and with anxious eyes sought through the darkness the place where the ranch buildings should be. All was silence. No report of firearms or whoop of savages disturbed the quiet of the valley.

Ascending a swell in the surface of the ground they saw that all the buildings had dis-

211

appeared, nothing meeting their anxious gaze but beds of lurid coals, occasionally fanned into a red glow by the intermittent night breeze. But there was the impregnable earthwork—the family must be in that! Randolph dashed swiftly forward, eagerly followed by his men. The earthwork was destroyed—nothing but a circular pit remaining, in the bottom of which glowed the embers of the fallen roof timbers.

A search for the slain was at once begun and continued for a long time. Every square rod of the valley for a mile was hunted over without result, and the party gathered once more about the two cellars in which the coals still glowed.

" It was in the cellar of the house that the boy said the body of his aunt was laid, was it not ?" asked Doctor Colton.

" Yes," replied Lieutenant Randolph.

" Then, if all were killed after he left—shot from time to time—would not their remains be likely to be beside hers ?"

" Not beside hers, I think. The last stand must have been made in the fort."

" Then the bodies must be under that circular bed of coal, Randolph, if they died here."

" Probably, doctor. It's an uncanny thing to do, but we must stir the coals and see. If all have perished, our duty ends here for the present; if they are living, we must find them. Sergeant Rafferty, have some fence rails brought and examine this pit."

In a few moments a half-dozen rails were being thrust down into the coals, their ends bursting into flame as they searched the fiery depths. Nothing was brought up.

"Randolph, didn't the boy say something about a covered way from this cellar to the spring?" asked the surgeon.

"That is so, doctor; they must be in that. Can you see any sign of an opening?"

"Nothing positive. Behind those wagon-tires there seems to be a natural slope of earth."

"Tip the tires over, sergeant," said the lieutenant, and presently a number of tires, from which the fire had burned the wheels, fell into the coals, disclosing a recently filled aperture.

"Looks as if the end of a passage had been filled, doesn't it?" said the doctor.

"It certainly does," answered the lieutenant. "Let us go down to the spring and examine."

The two officers and several of the men went to the spring. When they arrived there, Randolph and the doctor broke a way through the thick‑set willows into an irregular mass of small bowlders. Climbing over these they found themselves at the mouth of the passage, a little over five feet high and three feet wide.

"This must be the covered way," said the lieutenant. Placing his head within the entrance he called: "Oh, Mr. Arnold — we are here; your friends from Fort Whipple!"

"Thank Heaven!" in a man's tones came clearly through the entrance, accompanied by a sudden outburst of sobs in girlish voices.

"We'll be there directly," spoke another man's voice—that of a stranger.

Then followed the sound of steps, accompanied by voices, sounding at the entrance, as a voice spoken in a long tube appears to be uttered at the listener's end. Some time elapsed before those who seemed so near appeared; but at last there emerged from the passage Mr. Arnold, two strange men, and three girls—but no Brenda.

"Where's Brenda, Mr. Arnold?" asked Randolph.

"Heaven knows. She gave herself up to the Apaches."

"Gave herself up to the Apaches! What do you mean?"

"That's precisely what she did, lieutenant,"

214

said one of the strangers, adding: " My name is
Bartlett, from Hassayampa, and this is my
friend Gray, from La Paz. We were on our
way to Prescott, and stopped here for dinner.
But about the girl Brenda; she took it into her
head, after we got into the little fort, that unless some one could create a diversion to mislead the devils we'd all lose our scalps."

" That beautiful young girl! Give herself
up to certain torture and death? Why did you
allow it?"

" Wasn't consulted—surprised us. I hope,
lieutenant, you will not think so hard of me and
my friend as to believe we'd allowed it if we
had suspected what the plucky miss meant to
do."

" Tell me all the circumstances, Mr. Bartlett," said the lieutenant.

The party moved slowly along the path from
the spring to the fires, and as they walked Mr.
Arnold and the travellers gave an account of
all that had happened after Willie left for Fort
Whipple.

The burning arrows sent to the pitch - pine
roof became so numerous that the besieged
found it impossible to prevent the flames from
catching in several places. The boy was hard-

ly out of sight before the house became untenable, and the defenders were obliged to retire to the fort.

When the house was consumed and its timbers had fallen into the cellar, a mass of burning brands, the space about the earthwork was clear, and the rifles at its loop-holes kept the Indians close within the building they had occupied since the attack began. Not one dared to show himself to the unerring marksmen who watched their every movement.

For a long time silence reigned in the outbuilding. Not a shot came from its chinks, and the vociferous yells were still. But for the presence of their ponies and the two sentinels near the spring the defenders might have supposed the Indians had gone away. The whites, however, felt sure that plans were being matured which meant disaster to them.

At last these plans were revealed in a constant and rapid flight of arrows directed at a point between two loop-holes — a point which could not be reached by the besieged — and where, if a considerable collection of burning brands could be heaped against the logs between the earth and eaves, the pine walls and rafters must take fire. Walls and roof were too solid to be cut away, and water could not reach the outside.

The defenders held a consultation, and decided that in the event of the fire getting control of the fort they should retire into the covered way, block up the entrance with earth, and remain there until help should arrive. It was thought that the Indians would suppose all had perished in the flames.

"But they know we came here by an underground passage from the house," said Brenda. "Will they not suspect that we have entered another passage if we all disappear?"

"Perhaps they may," answered Mr. Arnold. "I had not thought of that. We'll have t' take our chances."

"If one of us was to appear to escape from here and join them," continued the girl, "I think they would suppose the others had perished and make no search."

"That may be true, but I'll take my chances here," said Mr. Gray.

"So will I," said his companion. "A fellow wouldn't last a minute outside this fort. I prefer smothering here to the death those devils would give me."

Time passed on, and it soon became evident

to the besieged that the outer wall was on fire. It was shown by the black smoke which wreathed in at the loop-holes on the northern side, and drew in long lines to loop-holes on the southern, and the fresh outbreak of whoops in which there was a note of exultation.

The sun had gone down and darkness was creeping over the valley when the first tongue of flame licked through a crevice in the roof and showed that the fire had gained a foothold. Soon a hole appeared close to the eaves, which gradually enlarged towards the centre of the roof and along the surface of the earth. With blankets the fire was beaten out on the sides, but it crept insidiously along between the timber and the earth covering.

In making the roof, branches of pine had been spread over the timber, and the branches in turn covered with a thick layer of straw to prevent the earth from filtering between the logs. This material was as dry as tinder, and held and carried the fire.

The men stood at the loop-holes and compelled the savages to remain under cover of the out-building, while the four girls exerted themselves to keep the fire from showing inside. Delay until help could arrive was what all struggled to gain. But the increasing heat and smoke showed the defenders at last that they could no longer put off retiring to the covered way.

The word was given and all entered it, and the men, with shovels, began to close the entrance. When it was a little more than half closed, the hole in the roof had become triangular in shape, resembling the space between two spokes and a felloe of a wheel. On the earth or felloe side of the triangle there was no fire; but the other sides were burning fiercely.

Making a sudden dash, and before any one could realize her intention, Brenda leaped past the shovellers, sprang over the embankment they were throwing up, and by the aid of a bench sprang up the four-foot wall through the flame-wreathed aperture and disappeared, her clothing apparently in a blaze. The war-whoops immediately ceased.

No attempt at pursuit or rescue was made. The Arnolds and their friends felt that it would be useless, and only result in the death of the pursuers. The work of closing the passage was resumed and completed, and all sat down in the darkness to await the slow passage of time and the possible arrival of the soldiers.

None of the party felt sure that Willie had succeeded in leaving the valley, believing, as they did, that his chances of passing the Apache pickets were few and desperate. They had more confidence in the supposition that Brenda's act would cause the Indians to believe all but the girl had perished, and lead them to depart at once with their booty.

After listening to the story of the Arnolds, Lieutenant Randolph concluded that Brenda had fallen a victim to the cruelty of the Apaches, and that a search would reveal her body mutilated and disfigured by her captors. A rapid and excited search was at once begun. Far and wide, over the plain, through the ravines, and into the foot-hills rode the soldiers, leaving no part of the country for two miles around unsearched; but not a trace of the missing girl was discovered.

Once more the detachment gathered near the ruins of the Arnold's home, and began preparations for returning to Whipple. The remains of the dead mother were lifted from beneath the charred timbers, and deposited in a grave prepared near by. While the burial was taking place, the two scouts, Weaver and Cooler, were absent, looking for the Apache trail. Day was dawning, and as it was probable when they returned that the command would start, the officer ordered the horses fed from the loose forage scattered about, and the men to prepare their breakfast.

The scouts returned as the men were dispersing from their meal, and Cooler placed in the lieutenant's hand a dainty lock of flaxen hair wound around the middle with another lock.

"I found it," said the scout, "beside the ravine yonder, a little more than two miles from here. The young miss is alive and dropped it for a sign. The redskins all left in that direction."

Whatever Brenda's three cousins may have lacked in education and cultivation, they lacked nothing in affection. They gathered about the little tress, took it daintily in their palms, kissed it again and again, and moistened it with tears. Low sobs and endearing names for the brave darling who had been willing to sacrifice her life to preserve theirs fell from their lips. Poor, rude frontier maids, they had shown an equal bravery all through the defence, and proved themselves to be worthy descendants of the race that lived through the colonial struggles with the Indians of the East. The three grief - stricken girls gathered about Lieutenant Randolph, and, clinging to his arms, besought him to go to the rescue of their cousin.

" Yes, yes, girls," he replied, " everything shall be done that possibly can be done. We will start at once, and I hope to bring her back to you. Mr. Arnold," he continued, " I will leave you a luncheon for the road, and you must try to make the distance to Prescott on foot."

" Yes, sir, we can cover the ground easy; thank you."

" I would leave you some of the men as escort, but in such an expedition I shall need more than I have."

" That's all right, Mr. Randolph. If I had a horse I'd go with you. There'll be no Apaches round this place for many days," and his eyes ran sadly over the ruins of his home, resting finally on the grave of his wife.

Yes, Brenda was alive, and a prisoner of the Apaches, spared by them, as children sometimes are after such raids, for adoption. It was plainly the duty of soldiers to rescue her from the cruel fate of a continued life with her captors.

IV

AFTER a delay sufficiently long to allow the scouts and their broncos to breakfast, the party mounted and turned to the west. Lieutenant Randolph asked Weaver to ride by his side, and questioned him about the country before them.

" I suppose you are familiar with this part of the country, Paul ?"

" Ought t' be; been here off and on since I was twenty."

" Have the Indians a camping-place near here ?"

" Yes; they spend a part of every year in this section, gatherin' *mescal*. From the direction they've took, I b'lieve they're goin' to Santy Maree Creek."

" That flows into Bill Williams Fork, doesn't it ?"

" Yes; and 't has a northern and southern branch. One of the favorite campin'-places of the tribe is on the southern branch."

223

" How far is it from Cholla Valley?"

" Fifty miles."

" Easy to approach?"

" Good ridin' all the way, 'cept a bit of bowlder country on a divide."

" Is the camp open to attack?"

" Wide open after you get into the valley. There's a water-fall, or, rather, a piece of rips there that 'll drown the noise of our comin'."

" Isn't it strange that Indians should camp in such a place?"

" They are Mescalero Apaches, and the *mescal* grows thick round there. ,Besides, there's no other place on the stream combinin' grazin' and waterin', and they've never been hunted into that region yet."

" Well, Paul, we'll try to hunt them there now if we have good luck."

The lieutenant urged the men on as fast as possible, taking care not to exhaust the horses and unfit them for a long pursuit. The soldiers were animated by a strong desire to punish the Indians for their treatment of the family in the valley, and were excited by the fear that the gentle girl in their hands might fall a victim to some barbaric cruelty before they could be overtaken, so that the animals

224

were constantly urged close to the powers of endurance. There was not much talking. Every pulse was throbbing with a desire to get within rifle-range of the savages.

There is no doubt but the Indian has been grossly abused, defrauded, and cheated since the white man first made his acquaintance. The scenes depicted in this story were the result of centuries of error and wrong on the part of Spaniards and, after them, Americans. Few army men are inclined to dispute this. The cruelty of the American Indian is the cruelty of every savage people, white or red, since time began. When on the warpath, to the savage mind it seems proper that no cruelty should be spared his victim. Whatever opinions, however, the soldier may entertain of the national method of conducting Indian affairs, it becomes his duty to secure peace by war when the resentful savage begins hostilities.

War with the Apaches, the result of gold-hunting and land encroachments upon their reservations, had been going on for several years. when the attack upon the Cholla Valley ranch occurred. The detachment now in pursuit of a band of the tribe entertained the natural resentment of a generous foe for a cruel and relentless one, and a personal acquaintance and warm, friendly interest in the family that had suffered animated the men with a strong resolution to administer severe punishment for what had been done in the valley.

Near the middle of the forenoon, as the soldiers were riding up a cañon, on each side of which rose rugged sandstone precipices, they came to a fork in the trail and the cañon. The track parted, and, judging from the footprints, most of the captured stock had passed to the right. Weaver said the right-hand path led to the northern branch of the Santa Maria, and the left to the southern branch.

The detachment halted perplexed. To divide the party of twenty-eight in order to follow both trails would be attended by much danger. To take the whole number over a wrong trail and not rescue Brenda was a course to be dreaded. Lieutenant Randolph called the scouts to him for consultation.

"Don't you think," he asked, "that it is probable a girl who was thoughtful enough to drop a sign to show she was alive and a captive would be likely to give us a hint which trail she was taken over from this point?"

"That's prob'ble, leftenant," replied Weaver.

226

"If you'll hold the boys here a bit, George and I will ride up the two trails a piece and look for signs."

"Go quite a distance, too. She might not get an opportunity to drop anything for some time after leaving the fork."

"That's true," said Cooler; "the redskins would be watching her very sharply. Which way will you go, Paul?"

"Let the leftenant say," answered the old scout, tightening his belt and readjusting his equipments for a longer ride.

"All ready, then," said Randolph. "You take the right, Weaver, and George the left. While you are gone we'll turn out the stock."

The scouts departed, and a few moments later the horses of the command were cropping the rich grass of the narrow valley, sentinels were posted to watch them and look for the return of the guides, and the rest of the men threw themselves upon the turf to wait.

An hour passed away, when Weaver was seen returning from the northern trail. As he approached he held something above his head. Directing the horses to be got ready, the officer walked forward to meet him, and received from his hand a small bow of blue ribbon, which he at once recognized to be the property of Brenda.

It now appeared certain the girl captive had been taken over the road to the right; so, without waiting for the return of Cooler, the men were ordered into their saddles, and the detachment started over the northern trail. It had not gone far, however, when a man in the rear called to the lieutenant. Looking back he saw the young scout galloping rapidly forward and beckoning them back.

A halt was ordered, and Cooler rode up to the commander and placed in his hand *a lock of flaxen hair bound with a thread of the same.* Placed by the other they were twin tresses, except that the last was slightly singed by fire.

Tears glistened on the eyelids of some of the bronzed veterans at the sight of the tiny lock of hair, and the accompanying reflection that the party had barely escaped taking the wrong trail.

"God bless the darlint," said grizzled Sergeant Rafferty, "there's not a redskin can bate her with ther thricks. We'll bring her back to the post, b'yes, or it 'll go hard with us!"

The sergeant's remarks were subscribed to by many hearty exclamations on the part of his fellow-soldiers. It was evident that the Apaches had expected to be pursued and had dropped the ribbon to mislead; and that Brenda, noticing the fork in the road and the division in the Indian force, and foreseeing the perplexity her friends would be in, had dropped her sign to set them right as soon as opportunity offered.

The lieutenant asked the guides if it was not probable the Apaches had a watch set on the overlooking heights to see which road his party took at this point.

"Sart'inly, leftenant, sart'inly," answered Weaver; "they're watching us sharp just now."

"Then we had better continue on the northern trail awhile and mislead them, you think?"

"My very thought. "That's the best thing to do. We needn't reach their camp until after midnight, and we might 's well spend the time misleadin' 'em."

"Yes; and it' ll be better to reach them near morning, too," added Cooler.

"Then we will go on as we began for some time longer," replied the lieutenant; and the soldiers again moved at a brisk canter over the northern trail. An hour afterwards a halt was made in a grassy nook, the horses turned out to graze until dusk, when the route was retraced to the fork, and the march resumed over the southern branch.

Night overtook the pursuers on a high ridge covered with loose, rounded bowlders, over which it was necessary to slowly lead the horses with some clatter, and many bruises to man and beast. The rough road lasted until a considerable descent was made on the western side, ending on the edge of a grassy valley.

At this point, Weaver advised that the horses should be left, and the command proceed on foot; for if the Indians were in camp at the rapids it would be impossible to approach mounted without alarming them; while if on foot, the noise of the rushing water would cover the sound of all movements.

Six men were sent back to a narrow defile to prevent the attacking party from being surprised by the Indians who had taken the northern trail, should they attempt to rejoin their friends at the rapids. Randolph determined, on the recommendation of the scouts, to defer making an attack until after three o'clock, for at that time the enemy would be feeling quite secure from pursuit and be in their deepest sleep.

The horses were picketed, guards posted, and lunch distributed, and all not on duty lay down to wait. Time dragged slowly. About one o'clock a noise on the opposite side of the creek attracted attention, and Cooler crept away in the darkness to ascertain its cause. In half an hour he returned with the information that the Indians who had taken the northern trail had rejoined their friends and turned their animals into the general herd. Upon learning this, the lieutenant sent a messenger to call in the six men sent to guard the narrow defile, and shortly afterwards they joined their waiting comrades.

An hour later Weaver announced the time to start. Leaving but one man to look after the horses the rest sliped down the slope into the river - bottom, taking care not to rattle arms and accoutrements, and began a slow advance along the narrow pathway, the borders of which were lined with the spiked vegetation of the country.

Going on for some time, Randolph judged from the sound of flowing water that they were nearing the camp. He halted and sent the two scouts to reconnoitre. They did so, and returned with the information that the camp was close at hand, and contained thirteen mat and skin covered tents or huts, and that the stolen stock and Indian ponies were grazing on a flat just beyond. No guards were visible.

The flat about the camp was covered with Spanish - bayonet, soapweed, and cacti, with here and there a variety of palmetto which attains a height of about twenty-five feet, the trunks shaggy with a fringe of dead spines left by each year's growth. Cooler suggested that at a given signal the trunks of two of these trees should be set on fire to light up the camp, and enable the soldiers to pick off the Apaches as they left their shelter when the attack began. He also proposed a yell, saying: " If you outyell 'em, lieutenant, you can outfight 'em."

Although the lieutenant doubted whether twenty-three white throats could make as much noise as half a dozen red ones, he consented to the proposition. He sent four men to the flat upon which the ponies and cattle were grazing, with orders to place themselves between the animals and the creek, and when the firing began drive them back along the trail into the hills.

When these instructions had been given,

Doctor Colton asked Randolph if the firing would be directed into the tents.

"That is what I was thinking of," replied the lieutenant.

"Of course Brenda is in one of them," said the doctor.

"Yes; and if we shoot into them indiscriminately we are as likely to hit her as any one."

"Can you think of any other way of locating her?"

"No; I am at a dead loss. We will try Cooler's plan of yelling, and perhaps that will bring them out."

He searched for Sergeant Rafferty, and directed him to forbid any one to fire until orders were given to do so.

V

ORDERS were passed and dispositions so made that one-half the force was placed on each flank of the camp. All movements were made at a considerable distance from the place to be attacked, and the utmost care taken to make no noise that would alarm the sleeping foe. Once on the flanks, the men were to creep up slowly and stealthily to effective rifle range. When the trunks of the palmettos were lighted all were to yell as diabolically as possible, and fire at every Indian that showed himself.

The front of the camp was towards the creek, which flowed over bowlders and pebbles with considerable rush and roar. The officer expected the Indians in their flight would make a dash for the stream, and attempt to pass through the shoal rapids to the wooded bluffs beyond.

The soldiers were told to screen themselves behind yuccas or the Spanish - bayonet, emole, and cacti. The lieutenant, accompanied by Paul Weaver, selected a clump on the northern side, from which he could observe the front of the tents. Sergeant Rafferty with George Cooler was on the opposite flank, and the lighting of a tree on the officer's side was to be the signal for one to be lighted on the other, and for the yelling to begin.

All was done as planned. The flash of one match was followed promptly by the flash of another. Two flames burst forth and climbed rapidly the shaggy palmettos, making the whole locality as bright as day. At the same instant the imitation war-whoop burst from vigorous lungs and throats.

ON AN ARIZONA TRAIL

Every one held his rifle to shoot the escaping Apaches; but not a redskin showed his head. The soldiers yelled and yelled, praetising every variation ingenuity could invent in the vain attempts to make their tame whiteman utterances resemble the blood - curdling, hair - raising, heart - jumping shrieks of their Indian foes, now so strangely silent. Not a savage responded vocally or otherwise.

But for the presence of the captive girl the attack would have begun by riddling the thinly covered shelters with bullets at low range. The Indians evidently understood that they were secure from injury as long as they kept out of sight.

The two burning trees had gone out, and two others had been lighted. It began to appear evident that if something was not done to bring out the foe, the supply of towering torches would be exhausted and nothing accomplished. In darkness the advantage might be on the side of the red men.

The surgeon, who reclined near the lieutenant, asked: "Do you think any of those fellows understand English?"

"Guess not; their neighbors are the Mexicans, and some of them know Spanish. You know we always employ a Mexican as interpreter when we talk with them."

" Then why not speak to Brenda in English, and ask her to try to show us where she is. The Apaches will not understand—will think you are talking to your men."

" Thank you, doctor. that's an excellent idea."

A soldier was sent along both flanks with orders for all yelling to cease, and for perfect quiet to be maintained. Then, acting upon the surgeon's suggestion, Randolph called in a clear, loud voice:

" Brenda, we are here, your friends from the fort. Your relatives are safe. Try and make a signal by which we can tell where you are. Take plenty of time, and do nothing to endanger your life!"

A long silence succeeded, during which two more palms were consumed, and the officer was beginning to fear that he would be obliged to offer terms to the Indians, leaving them unhurt, if they would yield up the captive and the stolen stock.

But before the lieutenant had fully considered this alternative Cooler approached from the rear and said: " Lieutenant, I've been creepin' along behind the wiggies, and I saw somethin' looks like a white hand stickin' out from under the edge of the tenth from the left."

" Show it to me," said the officer. " I'll accompany you."

Making a détour to the rear the two crept up to the back of the tent indicated, pausing at a distance of twenty feet from it. It was too dark to make out anything definite. A narrow white object was visible beneath the lower edge; that was all.

Cooler was sent back a short distance to light a palm, and as the flames crept swiftly up the trunk the officer saw by the flaring light a small, white hand, holding in its fingers the loose tresses of Brenda's hair. The question was settled. The captive girl was in the fourth tent from the right of the line.

Waiting until the fire went out, the two worked their way well to the rear.

" Go back, George," said Randolph, " to your flank, and tell Sergeant Rafferty to move his men to a point from which he can cover the rear of the camp, and open fire on all the tents except the tenth from the left and the fourth from the right. The rest of us will attend to those who run."

"All right, sir, we'll soon make it lively for the rascals."

"Light up some more trees when you are all ready."

"Yes, sir."

The lieutenant crept slowly back to his own flank and ordered a disposition of his party so as to command the space in front of the line of tents. In another instant the flames were ascending the two tree trunks, and the rapid crackling of rifles broke the early morning stillness. With the first scream of a bullet through the flimsy shelters the Indians leaped out and dashed for the river. Few fell. Rapid zigzags and the swinging of blankets and arms as they ran confused the aim of the soldiers. In less than five minutes the last Apache was out of sight, and the firing had ceased.

Concealment was no longer a necessary precaution, and the soldiers thronged the space before the tents. Walking to the hut from which he had seen the hand and tresses thrust out, the lieutenant called: "Brenda!" There was no response or sound. Looking into the entrance, he saw in the dim light of the awakening day the figure of a girl lying on her back, her feet extended towards him, and her head touching

238

the rear wall. The right arm lay along her side, and the left was thrown above her head, the fingers still holding her hair.

A terrible fear seized the young officer. He again called the girl by name, and receiving no answer went in, and, with nervous fingers, lighted a match and stooped beside her. He saw a rill of blood threading its way across the earthen floor from her left side. He shouted for Doctor Colton, and the surgeon hurried in. From his instrument-case he took a small lantern, and, lighting it, fell upon his knees beside the prostrate girl.

During the following few moments, while the skilled fingers of the firm-nerved surgeon were cutting away clothing to expose the nature of the wound, the lieutenant's thoughts found time to wander away to the girl's brother Willie, who had been left at the fort in spite of repeated requests to be allowed to accompany the detachment. He thought what a sad message it would be his province to bear to the lad if this dear sister should die by savage hands.

The lieutenant entertained little hope that the pretty girl could live. He looked upon her as already claimed by death. She who had made a long and weary march pleasant by her vivacity and intelligence was to die in this wretched hole.

But the skilful fingers of the young surgeon were continuing the search for some evidence that the savage stab was not fatal, and his mind was busy with means for preserving life should there be a chance. The officer watched, and assisted now and then when asked; waited with strained patience for a word upon which to base a hope.

At last the doctor dropped the hand whose pulse he had been long searching, and said: " She is alive, and that is about all. You see her hands, arms, and neck are badly scorched by the dash she made through the fire at the ranch. Then this wicked stab has paralyzed her. She has bled considerably, too. But she lives. Press your finger on this artery."

" Can she be made to live, doctor ?"

" The knife did not touch a vital part; but it may have done irreparable injury. I can tell more presently."

Nothing more was said, except in the way of direction, for a long time, the surgeon working slowly and skilfully at the wound. At last, rearranging her clothing and replacing his instruments in their case, he said· " If I had the girl in the post hospital, or in a civilized dwelling with a good nurse, I think she might recover."

"Can't we give her the proper attendance here, doctor?" asked Randolph.

"I fear not. She ought to have a woman's gentle care, for one thing, and some remedies and appliances I haven't here for such a delicate case. It is the long distance between here and the fort that makes the outlook hopeless. She cannot survive the journey."

"Then we will remain here," said the lieutenant, with decision. "Write out a list of what you want, and I will send Cooler to the fort for tents and supplies, a camp woman, Willie, and the elder Arnold girl."

"Randolph, you are inspired!" exclaimed the doctor. "We will save this girl. I'll have my order ready in a few moments, and then we will make Brenda comfortable. You and I can manage until a better nurse arrives."

A letter was written to Captain Bayard, the surgeon's memoranda enclosed, and a quarter of an hour afterwards Cooler was flying over the sixty miles to Fort Whipple. Three days later a pack-train arrived with the laundress, Willie and Mary Arnold, and with the stores and supplies necessary for setting up a sick camp. The wounded girl mended rapidly from the start.

On the fourth day succeeding the rescue Randolph returned to the fort with all but Sergeant Rafferty and ten privates of the detachment, who were left as a guard to the surgeon, his patient, and her attendants. The recaptured stock and captured Indian ponies were brought in, and Mr. Arnold was made even so far as oxen and horses went. He made no attempt, however, to return to Cholla Valley, but took an early opportunity to sell out his claim and everything belonging to it.

At the end of a fortnight Brenda had so far recovered as to warrant Doctor Colton in permitting her removal to Whipple. An ambulance was driven to the bowlder-covered ridge mentioned in a previous chapter, and she was borne upon a stretcher by the soldiers to where it stood in waiting. All went well, and on the second day after leaving the Santa Maria the invalid was comfortably settled at the fort.

In time Brenda fully recovered, and Gypsy and the handsomest pony captured from the Apaches were in almost daily requisition to take the young people on long rides about the fort and town. Letters were sent by Captain Bayard to their maternal relatives, and just before Christmas an uncle arrived at the fort and took charge of his nephew and niece, taking them and their ponies to his home in the East.

THE END

RETURN TO the circulation desk of any
University of California Library

or to the

NORTHERN REGIONAL LIBRARY FACILITY
Bldg. 400, Richmond Field Station
University of California
Richmond, CA 94804-4698

ALL BOOKS MAY BE RECALLED AFTER 7 DAYS

- 2-month loans may be renewed by calling
  (510) 642-6753
- 1-year loans may be recharged by bringing
  books to NRLF
- Renewals and recharges may be made
  4 days prior to due date

Lightning Source UK Ltd.
Milton Keynes UK
UKHW021655090219
336964UK00011B/1069/P